NOMAD

ACE OF SPADES

Creator & Author
REV TIM

Editor
GRACE ROSE

ISBN: 979-8-9998482-6-0
ISBN: 979-8-9998482-7-7

Table of Contents

INTRODUCTION

Book #1 that sets the stage for the Damon Legna™ series. For more books, quizzes, and information, please visit our website www.DamonLegna.com

A fictional story, any resemblance is purely coincidental.

A mix of Urban, Rural, and Suburban cultures.

When the world goes rogue, a former Tier 1 operator, and Combat Veteran puts his skills to good use. When he thinks he's alone, he's surprised by the presence of something other worldly. Almost angelic, with a twist of warrior. Hope you enjoy this. It's a life changer.

Godspeed,
Rev

ACKNOWLEDGMENTS
"Fair Use Notice"

All scripture references are from the website
BibleGateway.com

Another special thank you to 2ACC.org a 501(c)3
nonprofit charitable organization. For those aiming
to be more confident with Firearms, they offer
Targets, and Training through a less intimidating yet
effective peer-led approach. Practice with their basic
fundamentals curriculum, and enhance skills in
stressful and life threatening situations. For more
information visit www.2ACC.org

ABOUT THE AUTHOR

REV is an Ordained Minister, Certified Chaplain, and accomplished Small Business Owner, with a remarkable background as a highly trained (classified) Risk Management Specialist. He served an elite global clientele, including Celebrities, Politicians, Executives, Athletes, Entertainers, Dignitaries, and Clergy. Yet, his latest profound achievements are safeguarding the innocent.

Making the world a safer place for our future generations, should be at the forefront. Evil needs to be eradicated by any legal means necessary.

REV created the fictional character Damon Legna™ as a coping mechanism, after learning a loved one suffered abuse. Now, the mission continues.

1 - FIRST LIEUTENANT

The mist drapes Ironholler like a heavy curtain, softening the edges of the town's cobblestone streets and muffling the early morning sounds. It's October 2nd, and the air carries a sharp chill, the kind that seeps into your bones and makes you pull your jacket tighter. Napoleon Louis sits in the passenger seat of his sister's battered pickup, the engine's rumble a low growl beneath the hum of a country song on the radio. His duffel bag rests heavy on his lap, stuffed with everything he thinks he'll need for the life he's about to begin. The MEPS center looms ahead, a squat brick building with flags snapping in the wind, their colors muted by the fog.

His sister grips the wheel, her knuckles pale, her dark hair tucked behind her ears. She hasn't spoken since they left the house, but the silence between them is loud with unspoken fears. Napoleon stares out the window, watching the blurred shapes of Ironholler's houses and trees slide by, each one a timestamp of the life he's leaving behind.

"You sure about this, Napoleon?" she finally asks, her voice soft but threaded with worry. She glances at him, her eyes catching the faint light from the dashboard. "The military's not a game. It's... it's everything. Your whole life."

Napoleon shifts, the duffel bag creaking under his hands. "I'm sure," he says, though the words feel like stones dropping into his stomach. "I need this. Something bigger than Ironholler. Something that matters."

She sighs, a sound that carries the weight of their shared history, both parents died when they were kids, leaving just the two of them to lean on each other. "You're leaving a lot behind," she says, her voice catching. "Sarah, especially. You think she's gonna wait for you, out there fighting wars?"

Napoleon's jaw tightens at the mention of Sarah, his girlfriend since they were sixteen, sneaking kisses behind the bleachers at Ironholler High. Last night, she clung to him, her arms tight around his neck, her tears soaking his shirt as she whispered, "Come back to me, Napoleon. Promise you'll come back." He sees her face now, those summer-sky eyes, that laugh that could pull him out of any darkness. "I know," he says quietly. "But I'll come back. I always do."

His sister shakes her head, her lips pressed into a thin line. "You better. You're all I got left, you know that? Just... don't do anything stupid out there."

He reaches over, squeezes her hand, her skin warm against his calloused fingers. "I'll write. I'll call. Promise, sis."

The pickup slows as they pull into the MEPS parking lot, the engine idling with a low grumble. She turns to him, her eyes glistening in the dim light. "You better mean that," she says, her voice barely above a whisper. "I can't lose you too."

Napoleon nods as they hug goodbye, his throat tight. He steps out, the cold air hitting him like a slap, and slings the duffel over his shoulder. The glass doors of the center reflect the gray sky, and as he walks toward them, he feels Ironholler falling away, piece by piece, like leaves from a dying tree.

Inside, the MEPS center is a maze of fluorescent lights and clipped voices. Napoleon moves through the process like a man in a dream, signing forms, answering questions, standing for medical exams. A doctor with cold hands checks his pulse, his eyes, his reflexes, muttering, "Healthy as a horse." A recruiter, a grizzled man with a crew cut and a scar above his eyebrow, hands him a pen and points to the final line. "Sign here, son," he says. "You're about to become part of something bigger than yourself."

Napoleon signs, his hand steady, though his heart races. "What's next?" he asks, his voice low but firm.

The recruiter claps him on the shoulder, a grin splitting his face. "Welcome to the military, son. You're gonna do fine. Got that fire in you."

Napoleon nods, but his thoughts are already on the road ahead, on Sarah's tear-streaked face, on the sister he's leaving behind. "Thanks," he says, and the word feels hollow, like it can't carry the weight of what he's feeling.

The years blur into a relentless grind of sweat, dirt, and discipline. Basic training is a crucible, breaking him down and building him back up stronger, sharper, faster, as a Soldier. Napoleon pushes himself harder than the others, running extra miles, studying tactics late into the night, his Bible open beside him. He earns a spot in the Special Forces, the elite of the elite, where every mission is a test of will and skill. His body hardens, his mind sharpens, and by the time he's promoted to First Lieutenant, he's a leader, commanding a 52-man platoon called Ace of Spades.

The desert stretches endless before them, a sea of sand and heat that shimmers under a merciless sun. Napoleon stands at the head of his platoon, their gear clinking softly as they gather in a loose circle before their first combat tour as his unit. The air smells of dust and diesel, and the distant rumble of artillery underscores the tension. He holds his tattered Bible, its pages worn from years of reading, and opens it to Psalm 27.

"The Lord is my light and my salvation; whom shall I fear?" he reads, his voice steady, carrying over the wind. The men bow their heads, some clutching dog tags, others staring at the ground, their faces etched with nerves and resolve. "The Lord is the strength of my life; Of whom shall I be afraid? When the wicked came against me to eat up my flesh, my enemies and foes, they stumbled and fell. Though an army may encamp against me, my heart shall not fear; though war may rise against me, in this I will be confident!"

Marco, his sergeant, stands closest, his weathered face solemn. "Amen," he murmurs, and the others echo him, a low chorus that binds them together.

Napoleon closes the Bible, tucks it into his vest. "We go in, we do our job, we come out," he says, his eyes meeting each man's in turn. "Ace of Spades don't break. You hear me?"

"Yes, sir!" they shout, their voices a single force.

Marco steps forward, his grin crooked. "You praying us through this one, Preach?"

Napoleon's lips twitch, the nickname already taking root. "Somebody's gotta," he says. "Might as well be me."

The battle is chaos, a storm of gunfire and explosions that tear through the night. Napoleon leads from the front, his commands sharp, his focus unbreakable. They move as one, a machine of precision and violence, clearing enemy positions with ruthless efficiency. Bullets whiz past, mortars shake the ground, but Napoleon's voice cuts through it all, steady and sure. "Move left! Flank them! Hold the line!"

When the dust settles and the sun rises, painting the desert in shades of gold and blood, Napoleon gathers his men for a headcount. One by one, they sound off, their voices hoarse but alive. Fifty-two men went in. Fifty-two men come out. All unscathed.

Marco slaps his back, grinning through the grime. "You prayed us through, Preach. God's got your back."

Napoleon looks at his men, their faces etched with both exhaustion and relief. Feeling a surge of gratitude, he pulls a playing card from his pocket. The back contained a green pattern of suits, and the front was an Ace. The black spade stark against the white background. It's a symbol, the most powerful card in the deck. He holds it up, "Not just mine," he says. "All of us. Ace of Spades!"

The nickname sticks. Preach. It's more than a name now; it's who he is, a man of faith leading men through hell. But as they pack up their gear and prepare to move out, he glances at his watch. The time is 11:16. A chill runs through him, a memory from childhood, a pattern he can't shake. His mother's voice echoes in his mind, warning him about that number, the turmoil it always brings. He shakes it off, focuses on his men, but the unease lingers.

2 - 11:16

The desert doesn't care that the war is over. It stretches endlessly around the crumbling outpost, a sea of sand and heat that swallows everything, hope, history, even the bones of the military base itself. Scattered crates lie like relics, half-buried, their splintered wood bleaching under the glare. A storm brews on the horizon, dark clouds piling into towers, their edges jagged with distant strikes of lightning. The air hums with static, a tension that mirrors the pulse in Preach's veins as he stands at the center of the ghost town, his eyes scanning the distance.

Preach's fatigues are rolled to his elbows, the fabric stiff with dust and sweat. His dog tags clanging, catching the sun's dying rays. He stands a tall man, broad-shouldered, with a face carved by years of conflict, sharp jaw, eyes like chipped flint. He's seen enough to know the desert doesn't forgive, and neither does fate. He clutches a clipboard, its edges curling from the heat, and checks off the last of the inventory. Only five of them remain, a skeleton crew of Ace of Spades veterans tasked with shutting down this forgotten outpost: Preach, Marco, Plumber, Tech, and Demo. Their gear is pitiful, one M4A1 rifle, a single magazine, and two helicopters. One's new, bristling with armaments; the other's a patchwork, its frame scarred from years of service, held together by spit, prayers, and a mechanic's stubborn hope but it flies.

"We're almost done here, gentlemen" Preach says, his voice steady but rough, like gravel under boots. He wipes sweat from his brow, leaving a streak of grime. "One last sweep, then we're airborne."

Marco's sealing up a crate, his cap tilted back, revealing a shock of dark hair plastered to his forehead. He's younger than Preach, stocky, with a quick grin that hides the weariness in his eyes. "You taking the new bird, boss?" he asks, jerking a thumb toward the clean helicopter parked on the distant landing pad.

Preach glances at the chopper, its black hull shimmering in the heat. "Yeah," he says, scribbling a note on the clipboard. "You take the other raggedy antique. Don't want you denting my new ride."

Marco's grin widens, a flash of teeth against his tanned skin. "You're the one who flies like a damn maniac, Preach. I saw you in that training sim last month. Thought you were gonna spin us into the ground."

Preach's lips twitch into a rare smile, the tension in his shoulders easing for a moment. "Gotta keep you on your toes, gentlemen. Can't let you get soft."

From across the base, where the other three men are stacking crates, a chorus of chuckles rises. Plumber, a stocky man with a boxer's build and a perpetual squint, wipes his face with a rag. "Soft?" he calls, his voice thick with a Southern drawl. "In this heat? I'm melting, not softening."

"Speak for yourself," Tech shouts, tossing a water bottle to Demo. Tech's the youngest, barely twenty-one, with a boyish face and a knack for electronics that's saved their hides more than once. "Look at this baby face. I'm still pretty."

Demo catches the bottle, his massive hands dwarfing it. He's the quiet one, broad as a tank, with a shaved head and eyes that see more than he says. He grunts, uncaps the bottle, and takes a gulp, saying nothing.

Preach shakes his head, about to fire back a quip, when Marco's expression shifts. His grin vanishes, replaced by a tight-lipped frown. He raises his binoculars, the lenses catching the sun as he peers into the distance. "We've got company, Preach," he says, his voice low, tense. "Four vehicles, moving fast. Armed."

Preach drops the clipboard and climbs onto a crate, his boots scraping against the splintered wood. He shields his eyes blocking out the glare. Dust trails rise like smoke on the horizon, four plumes converging towards the base. He counts twelve men, insurgents, their silhouettes edged with rifles. One truck mounts a turret, its barrel ominous. "Find cover," Preach snaps, his voice cutting through the air like a blade. "Now!"

The men scatter, their boots pounding the sand. Plumber dives behind a stack of sandbags, Tech and Demo ducking into the shadow of a collapsed latrine. Marco grabs a rusted metal sheet, pulling it over himself like a shield. Preach snatches the M4A1 from where it leans against a crate, checks the magazine, thirty rounds, not enough, and slips into the shadows of the base. His Special Forces training takes over, his movements silent, deliberate. His heart is steady, his mind clear, but as he crouches behind a rusted out generator, he glances at his watch: 11:16. That number again, like a curse etched into his life. His mother's voice echoes in his memory, soft but insistent: *"When you see 11:16, Napoleon, brace yourself. Trouble's coming."*

The insurgents' vehicles roar closer, engines snarling as they skid to a halt fifty yards out. Bullets tear through the air, stitching craters into the sandbags and splintering crates. Plumber's voice rises over the chaos. "We're sitting ducks here, Sarge!"

"Hold tight," Marco calls back, his voice low but firm, barely audible over the gunfire.

Preach moves like a ghost, slipping between shadows. The insurgents are focused on the crates, their gunfire relentless, a storm of lead pinning his men down. He counts their positions, six near the trucks, four fanning out to flank, two manning the turret. They're disciplined, but not enough. Preach's eyes narrow, calculating. He needs to create a distraction, right now. He looks towards the old helicopter.

His men are defenseless to the relentless gunfire. Preach makes his move. Moments later, the whine of a helicopter engine spooling up catches the insurgents attention. Its blades slicing the air, kicking up a blinding cloud of dust. The insurgents freeze, their shouts rising in a mix of anger and confusion. They pivot, redirecting their fire toward the helicopter. Bullets ping off its hull, sparking against the patched metal.

Preach seizes the moment. The dust cloud cloaks the base, and the insurgents' attention is locked on the helicopter. He rises from a sand dune behind the enemy, smooth, silent, and fires. The first shot cracks through the air, dropping an insurgent with a clean headshot. Before the others can react, he fires again, and again, each bullet precise, surgical. One by one, they fall, their bodies crumpling into the sand. The turret gunner swings toward him, but Preach's shot catches him between the eyes. Twelve shots, twelve kills. The silence that follows is deafening, broken only by the dying whine of the helicopter's engine, its rotor blades slowing as bullet holes leak fuel into the sand.

Preach lowers the rifle, his chest heaving, sweat stinging his eyes. He steps out from the dune, scanning the base. His men emerge from cover, their faces pale, eyes wide with disbelief. Plumber's mouth hangs open, his rag dangling from his hand. Tech clutches a shattered radio, his usual smirk gone. Demo's gaze is steady, unblinking, fixed on Preach.

"Head count?" Preach yells, his voice calm but edged with steel.

Marco stumbles forward, his cap askew, his eyes tearing with awe. "All safe, you just saved our asses, Preach! How the hell did you take out twelve guys with headshots?"

Preach doesn't answer. He gestures to the new helicopter, its hull untouched by the firefight. "Let's move before more arrive."

They scramble toward the chopper, their boots kicking up sand. Plumber claps Preach on the shoulder as they climb aboard. "You're a damn machine, sir," he says, his voice shaky. "I owe you my life."

"We all do," Tech adds, sliding into a seat, his hands trembling as he buckles in. "That was... unreal."

Demo, settling into the back, says nothing, just nods, his eyes locked on Preach with a quiet reverence. "God was with you out there, Sir," he murmurs, almost to himself.

Preach slides into the pilot's seat, his hands steady on the controls. The blades spin up, a low thrum building to a roar as the helicopter lifts off, sand swirling below. He keeps his eyes on the horizon, where the storm clouds churn, lightning flashing in jagged arcs. The desert shrinks beneath them, its vastness indifferent to their escape.

Marco leans forward, his voice cutting through the engine's hum. "You didn't answer my question, boss. Twelve shots, twelve kills, all cranial on moving targets, how?"

Preach's jaw tightens, his gaze fixed on the storm ahead. "Training Sergeant," he says, his voice low. "And luck."

"Luck?" Plumber scoffs, leaning back in his seat. "That wasn't luck, Lieutenant. That was... biblical."

Tech laughs, a nervous edge to it. "What's next, Preach? We going back to reload?"

Preach doesn't smile. His fingers tighten on the controls, the helicopter banking slightly as he adjusts course. "Just getting us home," he says. "That's enough for now."

Marco raises an eyebrow, his cap still tilted back. "You okay, boss? You look like you saw a ghost out there."

Preach glances at his watch again: 11:32 now, but the memory of 11:16 lingers like a bruise. "Not a ghost," he says, his voice barely audible over the engine. "Just... a bad omen. That time, 11:16. Been following me my whole life. Every time I see it, shit hits the fan."

Marco frowns, leaning back. "You saying that number's cursed or something?"

"Not cursed," Preach says, his eyes narrowing as lightning splits the sky ahead. "Just trouble. It's the time both my parents died. Always means turmoil's coming."

Plumber lets out a low whistle. "That's eerie as hell, sir. You sure you're not cursed?"

Preach's silence is answer enough. Demo shifts in his seat, his voice soft but clear. "Maybe it's not a curse. Maybe it's a warning. God's way of telling you to get ready."

"Maybe," Preach says, but his tone carries no conviction. He doesn't believe in curses, but he can't shake the weight of that number, the way it seems to mark every disaster in his life. He flies on, the helicopter cutting through the air, the storm looming closer. Sand swirls in the distance, a haze that blurs the line between earth and sky.

Tech clears his throat, breaking the tension. "Well, whatever it is, I'm just glad you're on our side. I ain't never seen shooting like that, sir."

"Damn right," Plumber says, his grin returning. "That was some mercenary shit."

Preach's lips twitch, but he doesn't take the bait. "Focus, gentlemen," he says, his voice firm. "We're not out of this yet."

Marco leans back, crossing his arms. "You're no fun, boss. Saved our lives and won't even take a compliment."

"Let's just get to base," Preach says, his eyes scanning the instruments. "Then you can buy me a beer and call it even."

"Deal," Marco says, his grin returning. "But you're flying us straight through that storm, aren't you? Maniac."

Preach doesn't answer, but the corner of his mouth lifts slightly. The helicopter hums, carrying them toward safety, or whatever passes for it in a world that never stops testing them. Below, the desert stretches on, vast and unforgiving, its secrets buried in the sand. Above, the storm waits, its lightning a silent promise of more to come. Preach prays silently, asking for strength, for guidance, for whatever lies beyond the horizon. The time 11:16

burns in his mind, a shadow he can't outrun, a warning he can't ignore.

3 - HONORABLE DISCHARGE

Back stateside, this day was inevitable. A hard decision but one Preach had to make, it was time. He stands just beyond the base's main gate, his duffel bag slumped at his feet like a loyal dog waiting for its master. His chest beams with a constellation of medals pinned to his dress uniform, each one a story of blood, sweat, and survival. His DD-214 with Honorable Discharge tucked inside his jacket, crisp and official, but it feels like a paperweight against the years he's carried. The world is too quiet now, the constant hum of war, distant explosions, barked orders, the thrum of helicopters, replaced by the lazy chirp of cicadas and the occasional rumble of a passing truck. He squints against the glare, adjusting the brim of his service cap, and wonders how silence can feel so loud.

A shadow moves across the pavement, and Preach turns to see Marco approaching, his boots scuffing the ground with that familiar swagger. Marco's face is a map of their shared history, lines carved by years of combat, eyes that have seen too much but still hold a spark of warmth. His uniform is immaculate, but the way he carries himself, loose and unhurried, betrays the weight of their last tour together. He stops a few feet away, his hand extended, calloused and steady.

"You did good, Preach," Marco says, his voice rough as gravel but threaded with something softer, something real. "Hell, you did better than good. You kept us alive out there, more times than I can count."

Preach clasps Marco's hand, their grip firm, a silent language built over years of dodging bullets and pulling each other from the wreckage. "Couldn't have done it without you, Marco. You kept me grounded, Sergeant. From losing my damn mind."

They hold the handshake a moment longer than necessary, then step back, snapping crisp salutes in unison. It's their final one, and the gesture feels like a door closing. Marco's mouth quirks into a grin, but his eyes stay serious, searching Preach's face as if memorizing it.

"What's next, boss?" Marco asks, shoving his hands into his pockets. "You going back to that little town you're always yammering about? Ironholler?"

Preach nods, adjusting his cap again, the sun warm on his face. "Yeah. Haven't been back in years. Only place I can call home, though. You know how it is."

Marco's grin fades slightly, his gaze sharpening. "Family?"

"Just my sister," Preach says, his voice softening, the edges of his words worn smooth by memory. "Parents died when we were young. Basically raised her myself. She's all the family I got left."

Marco grips a hand on Preach's shoulder, strong, grounding. "Go see her, man. She's probably been waiting for you to show up and play big brother again." He pauses, his grin returning, sly now. "What about that girlfriend you used to talk about? Sarah, right? You still carry y'alls picture in your wallet?"

The name hits Preach like a stray bullet, sharp and unexpected. His chest tightens, a dull ache spreading beneath his ribs. He hasn't spoken of Sarah in over a year, not since her letters stopped coming. At first, he told himself it was the mail, lost in the chaos of war, misplaced by some overworked clerk. But as the months dragged on, doubt crept in, whispering that it might be something worse. He pats his pocket instinctively, feeling the worn edges of the photo he still carries, her smile frozen in time.

"Yep," Preach says, his voice low, almost lost in the cicadas' drone. "Sarah. Maybe something's still there. Great song, though. Might track her down and sing it to her one day."

Marco steps back, his grin softening. "You do that, Preach. And don't be a stranger. If you need anything, you know where to find me. Hell, I owe you my life, brother."

Preach nods, the weight of Marco's words settling into him. "Take care, Marco."

They hug, a quick, fierce embrace that says more than words ever could. Marco taps him on the back one last time, then turns and walks back toward the base, his silhouette swallowed by the gate's shadow. Preach watches him go, feeling the finality of it, like a chapter ripped from a book he's not ready to close.

He pulls out his phone, the screen scratched and scuffed from years of rough handling, and dials his sister's number. The line crackles, then her voice comes through, bright and startled, like sunlight breaking through clouds.

"Napoleon?" she says, her tone rising with disbelief. "Oh my God, are you okay?"

"I'm done," Preach says, crossing his arms, leaning against a nearby signpost as he lets out a long exhale. "Discharged today. Coming home for good. Don't tell anyone, alright? I want it quiet."

She laughs, a sound that warms him despite the miles between them. "My lips are sealed, big brother. You're gonna love it here, Napoleon. Things have changed, but... it's still Ironholler. Still got that same small-town heart." She pauses, and he can hear the smile in her voice. "Oh, and I'm engaged now."

"Engaged?" Preach's mouth curves into a grin, the tension in his chest easing for the first time all day. "You move fast, sis. What's his name?"

"Derek," she says, her voice softening, a little shy. "You'll meet him when you get here. And Napoleon? Be nice to him, okay?"

"Nice?" Preach chuckles, shaking his head. "When am I not nice? Come on, give me some credit."

"Uh-huh," she teases, her laugh bubbling through the phone. "You're all gruff and soldierly now, but I know you're still a softie underneath. You better not scare him off with that stare of yours."

They talk for nearly an hour, catching up on years apart. She tells him about Derek's job, about the new diner that opened on Main Street, about the way Ironholler's been holding its breath since the factory closed. Her voice is a lifeline, pulling him back to a world he left behind when he enlisted. When they finally hang up, Preach feels lighter, like Ironholler is already calling him home, its roots tugging at his soul.

He buys a bus ticket at a nearby station, the clerk barely glancing up as she slides it across the counter. The bus is half-empty, its seats worn and smelling faintly of cigarette smoke and stale coffee. Preach settles by a window, his duffel bag stuffed under the seat, and watches the landscape shift as the miles roll by. The flat, dusty plains of the base give way to rolling hills, their slopes blanketed in green. The air grows cooler, carrying the sharp scent of pine through the cracked window. He leans his head against the glass, his thoughts drifting to a memory he hasn't touched in years: an Ace of Spades playing card, a relic from his first tour. He'd carried it like a talisman, a reminder of luck in a place where luck was scarce. It's gone now, lost somewhere in the chaos of war, and he wonders if its absence means something, or if he's just being sentimental.

By the time the bus pulls into Ironholler, the sky is bruising into dusk, streaks of orange and purple smudging the horizon. The town feels both familiar and foreign, its streets unchanged, Main Street with its faded storefronts, the old oak tree in the town square, but its pulse is different, slower, like a heart that's grown tired. Preach steps off the bus, his shoes crunching on gravel, and takes a deep breath. The air tastes of home: pine, dust, and something sweeter, like the wildflowers that grow along the river.

A week later, Preach closes on a house at the edge of town, a modest two-story with a front porch and a big garage. It's more space than he needs, but it feels right, a place to rebuild, to carve out a life after the war. The yard is large and backs up to the forest, wild with knee-high grass and blackberry bushes, but he can already see himself fixing it up. Maybe building a shop in the garage. For the first time in years, he feels a spark of possibility, fragile but real.

His first mission though, is to find Sarah. He knows she works at the general store downtown, a fact his sister let slip during their call. The thought of seeing her sets his heart racing, a mix of hope and fear that makes his palms sweat. He stands in front of the mirror in his new bedroom, tugging on a clean white shirt and jeans that feel stiff compared to his fatigues. His belt buckle, polished silver, a gift from his father, contrasts against the denim. He pulls on his boots, the leather worn but sturdy, and settles a cowboy hat on his head, it's brim casting a shadow over his eyes. The reflection staring back at him is a stranger, a man who hasn't dressed as a civilian in nearly a decade. His shoulders are broad, swallowing the hat's silhouette, and his face is harder than he remembers, etched with lines that weren't there when he left Ironholler.

He climbs into his truck he bought off a neighbor for cash, and drives toward downtown. The streets are quiet, the kind that feels like it's waiting for something to happen. The general store comes into view, its sign faded but familiar, the windows stacked with jars of candy and fishing tackle. Preach parks across the street, his hands gripping the steering wheel as he stares at the door. The weight of the past presses against his shoulders, every letter he wrote to Sarah, every one she sent back, until they stopped. He doesn't know what he'll find inside, but the potential of her smile, the memory of it, drives him forward.

He steps out of the truck, the door creaking as it closes, and takes a deep breath. "Here goes nothing," he mutters, adjusting his hat one last time before crossing the street.

4 - SARAH

The general store in Ironholler is a living relic, its air thick with the scent of roasted coffee beans, aged pine shelves, and a faint dust that clings to everything like a memory. The aisles are a cluttered maze, stocked with canned peaches, dusty bags of flour, and fishing rods with handles worn smooth by years of eager hands. Fluorescent lights hum overhead, casting a pale sterile glow across the scuffed floor, where decades of footsteps have left faint trails. Napoleon steps through the creaking door, his boots thudding against the warped wooden boards, his heart hammering louder than his steps. He's traded his fatigues for a crisp country style, the first time in years he's dressed like a civilian, and the fabric feels foreign, stiff against his skin, like it's trying to rewrite who he is. His cowboy hat sits low, shading his eyes as he scans the store searching, his pulse quickening with every step.

Behind the customer service counter, Sarah stands, her blonde hair swept into a messy ponytail, a few loose strands clinging to the nape of her neck, catching the light like threads of gold. She's helping an older woman, her fingers deftly scanning a receipt, her smile polite but distant, her blue eyes, bright as the summer sky over Ironholler's rolling fields, focused somewhere beyond the transaction. Napoleon feels it before he sees her fully, a magnetic pull, like a current thrumming through his veins, whispering that she's near, the way it always has. His breath catches in his throat, and without thinking, he hums an old classic tune, the one that shares her name, the melody soft and low, barely audible over the store's chatter of voices, the rustle of shopping bags, and the occasional squeak of a cart's wheel.

Sarah's head snaps up, her pen freezing mid-signature, her eyes locking onto the stranger with the low hat. "Napoleon?" Her voice is a fragile whisper, almost lost in the hum of the store, trembling with disbelief. She squints as if she's trying to see through a dream, her lips parting slightly.

He takes a step forward, tipping his cowboy with a finger, just enough to reveal his eyes. Their spark catching the light like polished steel. "Hey, Sarah," he says, his voice low, rough with emotion, his throat pressed with years of unsaid words, each one heavy with the weight of deserts and battlefields.

Her pen clatters to the counter, and she vaults from her chair, her sneakers scuffing the floor as she rounds the counter, her steps quick, urgent, like she's afraid he'll vanish into the air. "Oh my God, you're home," she says, her voice breaking, and then she's in his arms, her body crashing into his with a force that steals his breath. He catches her, his hands finding her waist, steadying her as she wraps her arms around his neck, her legs around his waist, her body pressing against his like she's trying to make up for every lost moment. He breathes in her scent, lavender mixed with something sweet, like honeysuckle, and a faint trace of the store's dusty air. For a moment, they're teenagers again, sneaking out to the creek behind the high school, their laughter echoing under a starlit sky, the world theirs alone, untouched by war or time.

"You're really here," she murmurs, her face pressed against his chest, her voice trembling, muffled by his shirt and a trace of masculine cologne. "I didn't know if you'd ever come back, Napoleon. I hoped, I prayed, but I didn't know."

"I told you I would," he says, pulling back to look at her, his hands still on her waist, grounding them both. Her eyes are the same, endless and piercing, like they could see straight through him, but there's a shadow in them now, a weariness that wasn't there before, like she's carried too much in his absence. He notices a tattoo on the top of her foot, a delicate swirl of ink peeking out from her sneaker, black vines curling like a secret she hasn't shared. "You look... just like I remember," he says, his voice soft, honest, the words catching in his throat.

She laughs, a sound that's half-joy, half-nerves, and wipes at her eyes with the back of her hand, smudging her mascara into faint streaks. "Liar," she says, her voice teasing but shaky. "I'm a mess, all sweaty from this place, stuck behind that counter all day. You, though... you look like a soldier, Napoleon. All sharp edges and grown up. What happened to the boy who used to sneak me out past curfew?"

He grins, his hand lingering on her arm, her warmth seeping through her sleeve, grounding him. "Had to grow up sometime. You still stuck behind that counter, dealing with folks like her?" He nods toward the older woman, who's now tapping her foot impatiently, her lips pursed in a scowl.

Sarah glances back, her smile tightening. "Yeah, same old grind. Scanning receipts, dodging Mrs. Carter's complaints about expired coupons. You wanna stick around? I get off in an hour, maybe less if I sweet-talk my boss into letting me out early."

"I'll wait," he says, and he means it, not just for the hour but for as long as it takes. "Got some shopping to do." He fumbles through a rack of fishing lures, and watches her work. She moves with a rhythm, her hands quick and sure, her smile shifting from polite to genuine when she glances his way, a private look that makes his chest ache with a longing he's carried for years.

"Mrs. Carter, I'm sorry, but this coupon expired last month," Sarah says, her tone patient but firm, holding up the crumpled paper. "I can give you ten percent off, though. Store policy."

Mrs. Carter huffs, her glasses slipping down her nose. "That's robbery, Sarah. Back in my day, stores honored their customers, didn't nickel-and-dime them over a coupon."

"I know, I know," Sarah says, her smile tight but kind, her eyes softening. "Let me ring you up with the discount, okay? We'll make it right."

Napoleon watches, his lips twitching into a smile. She's always been good with people, smoothing over their edges, making them feel heard, even when they're unreasonable. He wonders how she's managed here, alone, while he was halfway across the world, dodging bullets and counting stars to keep himself sane, her face the only thing that kept the darkness at bay. He recalls looking at the moon, hoping she was seeing it too. A moment they could share no matter the distance between them.

When her shift ends, she grabs her purse, slinging it over her shoulder, and joins him outside. They sit on a weathered bench by the store's entrance, the evening air cool, carrying the scent of cut grass and distant pine. The sky is streaked with pink and gold, the sun sinking behind the hills, casting long shadows across the cracked pavement. Ironholler hums around them, the drone of a tractor in the distance, the laughter of kids racing bikes down the street, their shouts fading into the twilight.

"It's different now," Sarah says, her voice soft, her hands fidgeting with the hem of her shirt, twisting a loose thread between her fingers. "The diner got new owners last year. Changed the menu, got rid of the pecan pie. Everyone's pissed, you should hear them gripe. And the old mill shut down, so half the town's out of work. It became a public storage place. Things feels smaller now, like it's shrinking, or maybe I just notice it more."

Napoleon listens, his eyes fixed on her, taking in the way her lips curve, the way her fingers twist that thread like it's a lifeline. "Sounds like Ironholler's holding on by a thread," he says, his voice low, a faint smile tugging at his mouth. "What about you? You holding on?"

She shrugs, her eyes darting to the ground, her fingers stilling for a moment. "Trying to," she says, her voice quieter now, almost lost in the evening breeze. "It's been... hard. You were gone a long time, Napoleon. I didn't know if you were coming back, if you were even alive. Every day, I'd check the news, hold my breath, waiting for something awful."

He nods, the weight of her words settling in his chest like a stone. He wants to tell her everything, to pour out the years he's carried, but some things are too heavy, too raw. Instead, he shares what he can, the pieces that won't break him to say. "The war... it was nights under a desert sky so clear it hurt to look at," he says, his voice low, his eyes distant. "The men I led, their faces are burned in my head, but every last one of them made it home unscathed. The decisions I made, they still wake me up, sweating, in the dark. But you, Sarah... thinking of you, of coming back here, to this, to us... it's what got me through the worst of it." He pulls an old picture from his wallet. It was them together in high school, lovingly embraced.

Her eyes soften, a sheen of tears catching the fading light, and she reaches for his hand, her fingers warm against his calloused palm, her touch a tether to the present. "I never stopped loving you, Napoleon," she says, her voice trembling but sure. "Not for a second. Even when I didn't know if you were alive, I held onto you, like you were still right here."

He squeezes her hand, his heart swelling, the years apart shrinking to nothing in that moment. "Same here, Sarah. Always. Didn't matter how far I was, you were with me, every step."

They spend days together, falling back into each other like they never left. Her laughter fills his house, bright and warm, chasing away the silence. Her clothes spill across his closet, a tangle of colors mixing with his plain shirts and jeans. Her toothbrush sits beside his in the bathroom, a small, ordinary thing that feels like a promise. One night, they're in his backyard, the pool water lapping like small waves, the grass cool under their bare feet, the stars a bright canopy above, and crickets singing a chorus that feels like it's just for them. Napoleon drops to one knee, his heart pounding, a diamond ring in his hand, its band catching the moonlight like a beacon.

"Marry me, Sarah," he says, his voice steady despite the tremor in his chest, his eyes locked on hers. "I want forever with you. Every day, every night, just us."

She gasps, her hands flying to her mouth, tears spilling down her cheeks, catching the starlight. "Yes," she says, her voice breaking, a sob caught in her throat. "Yes, Napoleon, of course I will."

They kiss, sealing their vow, the stars bearing witness to their promise. Napoleon holds her close, her body fitting perfectly against his muscular frame, and for the first time in years, the world feels right, the pieces of his life clicking into place like a lock finally turning.

5 - ACE OF SPADES

The garage smells like a battlefield of creation: oil, sharp and slick, mingled with the acrid bite of fresh paint and the metallic tang of machined steel. Classic rock hums from a battered radio in the corner, its static-laced chords weaving through the clatter of tools and the low whine of a cooling fan. Preach stands in the center of it all, wiping his hands on a rag stained with grease and dreams, his gaze locked on the V-twin motorcycle that's consumed his nights for months. Its black paint gleams under the garage's honeycomb shop lights, chrome accents catching the glow like stars in a midnight sky. The gas tank is a canvas, adorned with a custom casino design, the words "ACE OF SPADES" standout in bold white letters that seem to pulse with defiance. This bike isn't just metal and horsepower; it's a testament, a piece of Preach's soul forged into curves and bolts, a machine born from sleepless nights and the need to prove he's more than the scars he brought home from war.

Sarah leans against the doorway, her arms crossed, a half-smile curling her lips as she studies the bike's sleek lines. Her denim jacket is frayed at the cuffs, her boots scuffed from years of riding horses. "Well, damn, Napoleon," she says, her voice warm, tinged with awe. "That thing's gorgeous. You've been holed up in here forever, haven't you? Tell me this isn't just a showpiece for you to stand there and admire."

Preach grins, the kind that crinkles the corners of his eyes, and tosses her a black helmet. "Maiden voyage's gotta be with you, darlin'. You know that."

She catches it with one hand, her eyes sparkling with mischief as she brushes a finger along the helmet's strap. "Better make it memorable, then. I'm no delicate flower, Napoleon."

He laughs, a deep, rumbling sound that fills the garage like thunder, and swings a leg over the bike, settling into the saddle. "Never thought you were."

Sarah slides the helmet on, her blonde hair spilling out beneath it, and climbs on behind him, her hands finding his waist with the ease of habit, as she leans against the backrest. The engine roars to life, a guttural snarl that shakes the concrete floor, and Preach feels it vibrate through his bones, waking something primal in him. He twists the throttle, and they peel out of the garage, the world blurring into streaks of color as they hit the roads of Ironholler.

The town slips past in a haze of tattered paint and sagging porches, the houses giving way to open country where the hills roll green and endless under a sky so blue it feels like you're submerged. Sarah's arms are tight around him, her laughter sharp and wild in his ear, and for the first time in years, Preach feels free. The weight of war, the ghosts that cling to him like smoke, slide off his shoulders, carried away by the wind whipping past. He reaches back, his hand finding her leg, giving it a gentle pat, a silent promise that this moment is theirs.

"Faster!" Sarah shouts, her voice bright with adrenaline, her fingers digging into his sides through his leather vest. "Come on, Napoleon, show me what this steed can do!"

He laughs again, the sound swallowed by the wind, and twists the throttle harder. The bike surges forward, the road unspooling beneath them like a black ribbon, the engine's growl a heartbeat in his chest. "You asked for it!" he calls back, his grin wide, the wind tearing at his words, his pulse hammering with the thrill of it.

They weave through curves, the bike leaning into each turn with a grace that feels alive, the world a streak of green and gold. Wildflowers sway in the fields, their petals catching the sunlight, and Sarah's laughter is a melody, sharp and sweet, cutting through the roar of the engine. Preach feels it deep in his core, a sense of being alive, of outrunning the shadows that have dogged him since he came home. The road, the bike, Sarah's arms around him, they're the only things that matter, the only things that feel real.

They pull into a gas station on the edge of Ironholler as dusk settles, the neon sign above buzzing faintly, its red glow casting long shadows across the cracked pavement. Preach cuts the engine killing the radio, the sudden silence heavy, and swings off to fill the tank, the nozzle clicking rhythmically in his hand. Sarah leans against the bike, her helmet tucked under her arm, her hair a wild tangle from the ride, strands sticking to her flushed cheeks.

"God, that was fun," she says, her voice bright, her smile wide enough to light up the fading day. "You built a monster, Napoleon. That thing's got a soul."

"Only the best for you," he says, winking as he pumps the gas, the sharp smell of fuel cutting through the evening air.

A voice, rough and loud, slices through the quiet. "Napoleon? Holy shit, man!"

Preach turns, and there's Kane, striding across the lot with a grin that shows too many teeth. He's broader than Preach remembers, his hair longer, tied back in a loose ponytail, a leather vest stretched across his chest with a "SLAYERS" patch across the back. Patches line the vest, symbols Preach doesn't recognize, hinting at a life that's veered far from their high school days.

"Didn't know you were back!" Kane says, clasping Preach's hand, his grip strong, his eyes bright with something that feels like nostalgia but carries a sharp edge. "Been some years."

Preach returns the handshake, his eyes scanning the vest noting the patches, the signs he doesn't know. "Good to see you, Kane. Been a while."

"Too damn long," Kane says, his grin widening as his gaze slides to the motorcycle. "That's a hell of a bike, man. Built or bought?"

"Twisted every bolt myself," Preach says, pride warming his voice as he rests a hand on the gas tank, his fingers brushing the Ace of Spades painted there.

"Go by Preach now, by the way. Picked it up in the war."

Kane nods, his eyes lingering on the bike, then glancing to Sarah. "Preach, huh? Suits you. And damn Sarah, you guys have been together since high school."

Sarah steps forward, her helmet still under her arm, her posture stiffening slightly. "Hey, Kane," she says, her tone friendly but guarded, her smile not quite reaching her eyes. "Yeah, I'm still putting up with him. Somebody's gotta keep him in line."

Kane laughs, a loud, barking sound that echoes across the lot. "Fair enough. Look, you two gotta come to our party tomorrow. Slayers' clubhouse, just outside of town on the old route. Can't miss it, big place, lots of bikes, lots of noise."

Preach glances at Sarah, catching the spark in her eyes, the way her lips curve like she's already imagining the night. "Sounds fun," she says, her voice lighter now, eager to be included. "What time?"

"Starts around eight," Kane says, clapping Preach on the shoulder, his hand lingering a moment too long. "Bring that bike, Preach. It'll fit right in with the crew."

Preach nods, his smile easy but his gut twisting with a faint unease he can't name. "We'll be there," he says, his voice steady despite the shadow creeping into his thoughts.

Kane's grin widens. "Sweet. Catch you tomorrow, man." He glances at his watch, then back at Preach. "Getting late, brother. Good seeing you again." They shake hands once more, Kane's grip firm, and he gives a nod before striding off.

Preach finishes filling the tank, the nozzle clicking off with a finality that feels heavier than it should. The price, $11.16 in total. He swings back onto the bike, Sarah climbing on behind him, her arms sliding around his waist again. As they ride home, the moon casts long shadows across the fields, the air cool against his skin. The excitement of the ride, the promise of the party, hums in his veins, a chance to reconnect with a past he thought he'd lost. But deep down, a number lingers in his mind, $11.16, a fragment of memory from a night in the war, a moment when everything went wrong. It's just a number, he tells himself, but it sits like an omen, a warning of trouble waiting to rise.

They pull into the garage, the bike's engine rumbling down to silence, and Sarah leans forward, her chin resting on his shoulder. "You okay?" she asks, her voice soft, cutting through the night like a blade.

"Yeah," Preach says, forcing a smile as he pulls off his helmet. "Just thinking about tomorrow."

She studies him for a moment, her eyes searching his, then nods. "It's gonna be good," she says, her voice firm, like she's willing it to be true. "You, me, and that beast of a bike. We'll show 'em how it's done."

He laughs, the sound softer now, and takes her hand as they head inside, the Ace of Spades resting under the shop lights, a symbol of who he is, and who he's willing to become.

6 - SLAYERS

The Slayers' clubhouse squats on the outskirts of Ironholler, a low, weathered building that looks like it's been standing since the town was born. Its walls are scarred with age, the air thick with the smell of beer, cigarette smoke, and the sharp tang of leather. Preach pulls up on the Ace of Spades, Sarah leaning against the backrest, the motorcycle's roar cutting through the night like a blade. The lot is packed with bikes, their chrome gleaming under the sign that reads "SLAYERS" in jagged letters. Music pulses from inside, a heavy bassline that shakes the ground, and laughter spills out, loud and raw, like the sound of men who live on the edge and don't care who knows it.

Kane greets them at the door, his grin wide, a beer in his hand, his leather vest worn proudly. "Preach! Sarah! Welcome to the den!" He's in his element, the president of the Slayers, a group of 1%ers with a reputation that makes the locals whisper and cross the street. He pulls Preach into a half-hug, slapping his back. "Man, it's good to have you here Brother. Come on, meet the crew."

Inside, the clubhouse is a haze of smoke and noise, the air warm with the press of bodies and the sharp bite of whiskey and weed. The walls are plastered with photos, flags, and motorcycle parts, a carburetor mounted like a trophy, a rusted chain draped like a garland, a shrine to the Slayers' life. The floor is sticky with spilled beer, the tables scarred with knife marks and cigarette burns. Kane leads them through the crowd, his voice booming over the music as he introduces Preach to the ten other members, their faces hard but curious, their vests marked with patches that tell stories of loyalty, blood, and defiance.

"This is Preach," Kane says, his voice carrying over the pounding rock song blaring from a speaker in the corner. "Local war hero. Ace of Spades platoon. Badass motherfucker."

The men nod, some raising their beers in respect, their eyes sizing him up, weighing his worth. A few mutter greetings, their voices rough, their gazes lingering on the scars peeking from Preach's sleeves, the marks of a man who's seen more than they'll ever know. Kane points to two identical twins, lean and sharp-eyed, both their vests marked with "Vice President" patches, their faces like mirrors of each other. "This is Case and Chase, the wonder twins" he says. "They keep things running smooth."

Case steps forward, shaking Preach's hand, his grip firm, his eyes assessing, like he's looking for a crack in Preach's armor. "Heard about you," he says, his voice low, measured, the kind of voice that doesn't give anything away. "Ace of Spades, huh? That's some serious shit."

Preach nods, matching his intensity, his own gaze steady. "Just did my job."

Chase smirks, sizing him up, his eyes beaming with a challenge. "You ride like you fight?"

"Better," Preach says, his voice calm but edged, and the twins laugh, a sound that's both welcoming and testing, like they're trying to see how far they can push him.

Sarah stays close, her hands around Preach's muscular arm, her smile tight, her eyes darting around the room. "You boys always this intense?" she says, her tone light, trying to cut through the tension, but her fingers tighten on Preach's arm, betraying her unease.

"Only when there's a war hero in the room," Chase says, winking, but there's an edge to it, a sharpness that makes her fingers dig deeper into Preach's sleeve.

Kane leads them to a wall covered in photos, pointing to one of their high school football team, young and invincible, their helmets gleaming under stadium lights, their grins wide and carefree. "Remember this night Preach? We were kings back then," Kane says, his voice thick with nostalgia, his finger tapping the glass. "You, me, tearing up the field. Still are, in our own way."

Preach studies the photo, his younger self staring back, a boy untouched by war, his arm slung around Kane's shoulders, Sarah, a young cheerleader jumping in the background. "Yeah," he says softly, his voice thick with memory. "Feels like a lifetime ago. That was a great Homecoming win."

"Shit changes, man," Kane says, his eyes distant, his hand lingering on the frame. "But some things don't. You're still one of us, Preach."

Sarah shifts beside him, her hand slipping from his arm, her posture stiffening. "Oh God I looked so young back then, now I need a drink," she says, her voice bright but strained, her eyes avoiding his. "You boys catch up."

Preach watches her go, her silhouette weaving through the crowd, her ponytail swaying, and feels a pang he can't name, a bit of unease that he pushes down. The night blurs by with whiskey and laughter, the room spinning, the music loud in their ears. Sarah dances with Preach, her body close, her hands on his shoulders. Her eyes looking into his as they were the only two people in the room, caught up in the haze of smoke and alcohol. Magnetized by the pull of the past.

They make their way over to the bar once again. "Another shot?" Sarah asks, holding up a glass, her cheeks flushed, her smile wide but brittle.

"Hell yeah," Preach says, clinking his glass against hers, the burn of whiskey grounding him in the chaos, the room a swirl of smoke and noise.

Kane pulls him aside, his tone serious, his breath heavy with booze. "You're welcome here anytime, man," he says, his hand on Preach's shoulder, his eyes searching. "We could use someone like you in the Slayers. You've got the grit, the balls, Brother. Think about it."

Preach claps his shoulder, his mind foggy but his instincts sharp, a flicker of doubt beneath the whiskey's haze. "Appreciate it, Kane. You've got something good here man, I'll give it some thought."

Sarah and Preach stumble out the door. They ride home, the night air cool against their flushed skin, Sarah's arms loose around his waist, her laughter quieter now, subdued. They arrive home safely, tucking the Ace of Spades into the garage for the night. They collapse into bed, the world fading to black, their bodies tangled in loving nostalgia, the clubhouse's noise still ringing in their ears.

The next morning, Preach wakes with his head hanging off the edge of the bed, the room tilted at an odd angle, his mouth tasting like stale whisky, his head pounding like a drum. He focuses on the digital clock on the dresser: 91:11. He blinks, turns right-side-up, and sees it clearly: 11:16. His heart skips, that number a shadow that follows him, a warning he can't shake.

Sarah stirs, her head on his bare chest, her breath warm against his skin, her voice thick with sleep. "What's wrong, baby?" she murmurs, her hand resting lightly on his arm.

"That time," Preach says, his voice low, his heart racing, the number burning in his mind. "11:16. Every time I see it, some turmoil happens. Always has."

She laughs softly, kissing his chest, her lips warm and gentle. "Well, last night we created turmoil in this bed, baby," she says, her voice teasing, trying to lighten the moment.

Preach chuckles, the tension easing, her warmth pulling him back from the edge. "That was turbulence, my love. Two very different things."

She giggles, climbing onto his back as he heads for the shower, her arms around his neck, her legs dangling. "Gimme a piggyback ride," she says, her voice bright, playful, and he carries her, their laughter echoing through the house, a fleeting moment of lightness before the storm he thinks is coming.

7 - WRECKED

The sun blazes high over Ironholler, painting the rolling hills in shades of gold and green as Preach leans into a curve, the Ace of Spades humming beneath him. The motorcycle's rumble is a steady pulse, a counterpoint to the wind whipping past, carrying the scent of pine and warm asphalt. He squints against the glare, his leather jacket creaking, his thoughts drifting to the life he's building. A new home, this bike, and most importantly, Sarah. The woman of his dreams, her laughter still vivid in his mind from their high school days, her touch a promise of forever. He lets a rare smile slip, picturing a future that feels close enough to grasp. *Imagine me being a dad?* The thought sparks warmth in his chest, a dream he's carried since he was a kid himself, running wild through these same hills. A family, a legacy, something real.

He pulls into the garage, the Ace of Spades' growl fading into the afternoon's quiet. The house looms still, too empty without Sarah's presence. She's still at the store, her shift dragging on, and Preach feels the silence like a weight. He steps inside, the hardwood under his boots, and surveys the living room. Cardboard boxes are stacked haphazardly, Sarah's belongings spilling out like secrets she hasn't shared. She's been putting off unpacking, always finding an excuse, but Preach wants her to feel at home. This is their place now, a foundation for the life they're supposed to build together. He kneels beside a box, slicing through tape with his pocketknife, and begins pulling out her things, paperback novels with creased spines, a scarf that smells faintly of her lavender perfume, a chipped coffee mug from some diner years ago.

One box yields a photo album, its leather cover worn soft from handling. He hesitates, then opens it, the pages crinkling under his fingers. The photos hit him like a punch, high school memories frozen in time. There's Sarah in her blue prom dress, her hair pinned up, laughing as he fumbles with his rented tux. Another of them by the lake, feet dangling in the water, her head tilted against his shoulder. A football game, her cheering from the sidelines, his number 33 painted on her face. He traces a finger over a photo by the creek, her eyes bright, his grin wide and unguarded. They were kids then, untouched by the world's sharper edges. His heart aches, a mix of nostalgia and longing for that simplicity.

He sets the album aside, the memories lingering like a song he can't shake, and moves to another box. This one feels heavier, more secretive, as if it's been packed to hide something. Inside, he finds a folded piece of thin paper, its edges crisp and clinical. An ultrasound from years ago. Sarah's name is printed at the top, the date April 5th. Seven months after he deployed. The baby was eight weeks along. His hands shake, the paper trembling as he sets it on the kitchen table. His breath catches, a sharp pain slicing through his chest. He digs deeper, driven by a need to understand, and finds a stack of photos. Sarah, her smile soft and intimate, kissing a man who isn't him. The images searing, her lips on his, her hands in his hair, a moment that was supposed to belong to Preach alone.

Another box, another wound. Health records, stark and undeniable, confirming an abortion in May. The dates align, a timeline of betrayal that clicks into place with devastating clarity. Seven months after he left, she was with a new guy, and got pregnant. A void flooded into his heart. The dream he'd held, of a family, of her carrying his child, shatters like glass under a rock. His life, the one he thought he was coming home to, is now a pile of wreckage.

Preach lays the ultrasound, the photos, and the records on the kitchen table, arranging them like evidence in a trial. His hands are steady, but his chest is tight, the air sucked from his lungs. The house is silent except for the faint tick of the clock on the wall, each second a hammer against his heart. The tinnitus in his ears ringing, a remnant of his time overseas, but it's drowned by the roar of his thoughts. He steps outside to the backyard, the pool shimmering under the late afternoon sun, its surface deceptively calm. He strips to his shorts, the air warm against his skin, and dives in. The water is cool, a shock that cuts through him, each stroke a way to channel the rage building inside, the hurt threatening to tear him apart. He swims, the rhythm of his strokes relentless, trying to drown the pain, to keep it from consuming him.

Sarah's keys jangle as she steps through the front door, her voice calling out, "Napoleon?" It's soft at first, then stops short. He hears her footsteps falter, the clatter of her purse hitting the floor. She's seen the table, the photos, the ultrasound, the records laid out like a crime scene. Her breath hitches, a sound that carries through the open patio door. She steps outside, her flip-flops slapping against the concrete, her silhouette framed against the light.

"Napoleon," she says again, her voice trembling, thick with panic. She clutches the ultrasound, her knuckles white. "Please, let me explain."

He keeps swimming, his strokes deliberate, cutting through the water like he's fighting something bigger than himself. The pool is his refuge, a place to contain the storm inside. She kneels by the edge, her hands gripping the concrete, her eyes red and watering. "Napoleon, please," she pleads, tears streaming down her face. "Just talk to me. I didn't mean for this to happen."

He ignores her, his focus on the rhythm, the burn in his muscles, anything but her voice. She stands, her voice rising, raw and desperate. "You left me!" she screams, the words echoing across the water, sharp enough to slice through his resolve. "I was lonely, Napoleon! I didn't know if you were coming back! You were gone, everything was falling apart, and I didn't know what to do! Talk to me, damn it! Please!"

He stops at the edge of the pool, his hands gripping the lip, water streaming from his shoulders. His eyes lock onto her foot, the delicate swirl of ink, a tattoo he found mysterious, a small rebellion she'd gotten after high school. But now, in the fading light, he sees what he missed before: faint track marks, barely hidden by the ink, signs of IV drug use he'd been too blind to notice. His love had clouded his vision, painted her as the girl he'd always known, not the woman standing before him now. "You betrayed me," he says, his voice low, cold, final, cutting through her sobs like a blade.

Sarah sinks to her knees, her hands covering her face, her body shaking. "It was Kane," she whispers, her voice barely audible, choked with tears. "He... he gave me the drugs. I didn't mean to, Napoleon. I was lost, and he was there, and I... I got pregnant. I couldn't keep it. I couldn't. I'm so sorry."

He stands, water dripping from him, pooling at his feet. His face is a mask of pain, his eyes burning with hurt, with the weight of a future stolen. "All I ever wanted was a family, with you," he says, his voice breaking, each word raw and heavy. "Kids, a home, a life together. That dream's gone now, Sarah. Wrecked forever."

She cries harder, her words a jumbled plea, her hands reaching for him, grasping at air. "I love you, Napoleon. I messed up, I know it was a mistake, but I love you. Please, don't do this. Don't leave me again, please!"

"It's done," he says, his voice hard, his eyes empty, the man she knew replaced by something colder, forged in the fire of her betrayal. "I'm not the one leaving this time. Get your shit and get out of my house. For good."

Sarah's sobs grow louder, echoing through the open door as she stumbles back into the house. Her footsteps are frantic, her cries muffled by the walls as she gathers her things, the sound of zippers and rustling fabric a counterpoint to the silence that follows. Preach dives back into the pool, the water swallowing his rage, his grief, his shattered dreams. He swims until his muscles scream, until the world is nothing but the rhythm of his strokes, but the pain doesn't fade, a wound that won't close.

Hours later, the house is dark, the silence oppressive. His phone buzzes on the kitchen counter, cutting through the quiet like a siren. It's Keisha, his sister. He answers, "Hey sis, what's up?"

Her voice tight with urgency. "Napoleon, I have to tell you something, It's about Sarah."

Preach interrupts her, "Sis, I don't want to hear anything about her, she betrayed me and I..." Keisha stops him suddenly.

"Napoleon, she overdosed. She's here at Ironholler Hospital in critical condition. I was working triage when they brought her in. They don't think she's going to make it."

"What?" Preach hangs up and bolts out the door. He's on his bike in seconds, the Ace of Spades roaring to life, the road blurring beneath him as he races through the night, wind biting at his face. The hospital looms ahead, its lights stark against the darkness. He runs in, and Keisha brings him directly to Sarah in the ICU. Tubes snaking from her arms, her face pale, she's on a respirator breathing shallow, almost nonexistent. He sits by her bedside, taking her hand, her skin cold against his. "Sarah," he whispers, his voice thick, searching for some sign of life, some spark of the woman he loved. "Come on, stay with me. You gotta fight." He's not leaving her side.

In the middle of the night, the heart monitors erupt, beeping frantically, alarms piercing the quiet. Preach jumps to his feet, still clutching her hand, his pulse racing. A single tear rolls down her cheek, glistening under the fluorescent lights, and then the monitors flatline, a single, endless tone that stops his heart. Doctors and Nurses rush in, their voices sharp, urgent, pushing him aside. "Sir, you need to leave the room," one says, her hands already moving, preparing to fight for Sarah's life.

He stumbles into the hallway, his breath fogging the glass window as he watches them work, their movements a blur of efficiency. Chest compressions, a defibrillator's hum, shouted orders, life fighting to hold on. The monitors start beeping again, a fragile rhythm returning, and Preach exhales, his hands trembling. The doctor steps out, his face grim, his eyes shadowed with fatigue. "She's in bad shape," he says, his voice low, steady. "Brain damage, likely from the overdose. She'll need long-term inpatient rehab, and even then, recovery's uncertain."

"Do whatever it takes," Preach says, his voice steady despite the storm inside, the rage and grief warring with the need for her to survive. "You save her."

The doctor nods, glancing at his chart. "What's your relationship to the patient, sir?"

"I'm her fiancé," Preach says, the words heavy, a truth that no longer fits but still binds him to her, a chain he can't break.

"Okay, we'll keep you posted on her progress." The doctor walks away, leaving Preach alone in the hallway, his rage simmering, a dangerous heat building in his chest. Kane did this. Got her hooked, broke her, broke them. His fists clench, his knuckles white, his mind set on a single truth: Kane will pay, one way or another.

8 - THE STORM

The Slayers' clubhouse squats on the edge of Ironholler like a beast waiting to pounce, its walls stained with years of smoke and neglect. The late morning sun beats down, turning the asphalt lot into a shimmering haze, the air thick with the scent of exhaust and stale beer. The sign above the door, its letters faded to a dull gray, hangs silent in the daylight, as if the place is holding its breath. Preach's Ace of Spades roars up the road, its engine a guttural snarl that echoes the storm churning within him. His blood is molten, his hands tight on the grips, his jaw clenched so hard his teeth ache. Sarah's face, her hollow eyes, her trembling confession, burns in his mind, and every mile he's ridden has only stoked the fire.

He pulls into the clubhouse parking lot and cuts the engine. The sudden silence deafening, and swings his leg over the bike. His boots hit the ground with a heavy thud, kicking up a puff of dust. The clubhouse door looms ahead, its chipped paint peeling like old skin. Preach doesn't knock. He doesn't pause. He shoves the door open, the hinges screaming, the wood slamming against the wall with a crack that splits the quiet inside.

The room smells of sweat, whiskey, and something sour, like regret left to fester. Kane lounges at a table near the bar, a beer bottle sweating in his hand, his leather vest over him like armor. Case and Chase, the twins, flank him, their identical smirks sharp as knives. They're laughing, their voices loud and careless, until Preach's shadow falls across the room. The laughter dies.

Preach doesn't speak. His fist does. It cuts through the air, a missile of bone and rage, and connects with Kane's jaw. The crack is sharp like a gunshot in the dim room. Kane flies backward, his chair tipping, his body crashing over the table. Bottles shatter on the floor, glass exploding across the sticky wood, the amber liquid pooling like blood.

"What the fuck, Preach?" Kane roars, scrambling to his feet, his hand wiping at the blood trickling from his split lip. His eyes blaze, dark and dangerous, his body coiled like a snake ready to strike.

Case and Chase are on Preach in an instant, their hands like vises on his arms, pinning him back. Case's grip is brutal, his fingers digging into Preach's bicep, his breath hot and sour against Preach's ear. "You lost your damn mind, man?"

Chase leans in, his face a mirror of his brother's, his voice low and mocking. "You think you can just walk in here and start swinging?"

Preach strains against them, his muscles taut, his Special Forces training screaming to break free, to turn their holds into leverage, to snap their wrists like twigs. But Kane waves them off, his voice a low growl, his eyes locked on Preach's. "Let him go. Outside, now!"

The twins release him, their hands lingering just long enough to make a point. Preach shakes them off, his chest heaving, and follows Kane through the door. The lot outside is a furnace, the sun searing the back of his neck, the air heavy with the tang of gasoline and dust. The four men stand in a loose circle, the tension between them a living thing, crackling like the storm Preach knows is coming.

Preach rounds on Kane, his voice shaking with rage, each word a bullet fired point-blank. "You stole her, Kane. My Sarah. Got her hooked on that poison. You piece of shit."

Kane's eyes narrow, his stance wide, his hands balling into fists at his sides. "You're wrong, Preach. Dead wrong. She came to me. Knocked on my door, eyes all wild, begging for a hit. I didn't drag her into anything. She wanted the fast life. She chose it."

Preach's heart stumbles, but he doesn't flinch. "You're fucking lying," stepping closer, his boots crunching on the gravel. "You saw her, saw she was mine, and you took her. Fed her that shit till she couldn't think straight."

Case stands tall, his arms crossed, a smirk curling his lips like smoke. "She likes to party, man. With all of us. You didn't know? Your girl's got a taste for the wild side."

Chase laughs, the sound sharp and cruel, his eyes filled with malice. "Yeah, Preach, she's been having a real good time. You think you're gonna save her? Put a ring on it? Shit, man, she's been partying with us for years."

Kane's grin is cold, his voice dripping with venom. "Oh, guys, he's trying to turn a meth whore into a housewife."

The twins erupt in laughter, their voices grating, mocking, slicing through Preach like shrapnel. The words hit harder than any fist, each syllable a betrayal, a confirmation of the truth he's been dodging. Sarah's voice echoes in his head, *I didn't mean to, Preach, I just... I needed it*, and the world goes red.

Preach lunges, his body a weapon, his fists and feet moving with the precision of a man trained to kill. He lands a hook on Kane's cheek, the impact like a brick. Case swings, but Preach ducks, his elbow slamming into Case's jaw, sending the twin stumbling. Chase charges, and Preach meets him with a knee to the ribs, the air rushing out of Chase's lungs in a grunt. The fight is chaos, a storm of punches and curses, boots skidding on gravel, blood mixing with sweat. Preach is a machine, his Special Forces instincts taking over, his body moving faster than thought, fueled by betrayal, by the image of Sarah's face in the hospital, pale and broken.

A police cruiser rolls into the lot, its lights flashing red and blue, cutting through the haze of violence. Officer Baker steps out, his hand resting on his holster, his eyes scanning the scene with a calm authority that belies the tension in the air. His uniform crisp despite the heat, his badge catching the sunlight.

"Problem here, fellas?" Officer Baker asks, his voice firm but even, his gaze moving from Preach's knuckles to the blood on Kane's face.

Kane wipes his lip, forcing a smile that doesn't reach his eyes. "No, Officer Baker. This guy was just leaving."

Preach's chest heaves, his breath ragged, but he doesn't break eye contact with Kane. Officer Baker's gaze shifts to him, narrowing slightly, his hand still on his holster. "Don't shit where you eat, guys. I don't want to see this kind of activity in Ironholler again. You hear me?"

"10-4, Officer Baker," Kane says, his tone smooth, his smile tight as a drum. "You won't have a problem from us."

Preach glares at Officer Baker, his eyes burning with a mix of defiance and rage. He doesn't trust the cop, doesn't trust the way his hand hovers near his gun, the way his eyes linger just a little too long. Without a word, Preach turns, his boots heavy on the ground, and mounts the Ace of Spades. The engine roars to life, a primal scream that drowns out the echo of Kane's laughter, the sting of Case and Chase's taunts. He meets Kane's eyes one last time, and the promise there is clear: this isn't over.

"See you soon, Preach," Kane calls, his voice a hiss, his smile cold as ice.

Preach twists the throttle, the bike surging forward, the wind sharp against his face, cutting through the fog of anger and betrayal. The words "meth whore" loop in his mind, each one a needle in his skin. He rides hard, the road blurring beneath him, Ironholler fading into a smear of gray and green. Sarah's face haunts him, her voice a ghost in his ear, and he wonders if he ever really knew her at all.

Later, on the edge of town, the world feels different. The outdoor shooting range stretches out before him, a barren strip of dirt, wood, and steel, the horizon wide and unforgiving. Preach sets up his stages, special 2ACC.org targets, numbered 001, 116, and 138. Their outlines stark against the pale sky, like ghosts of enemies he's faced before. He checks his silenced pistol, the weight familiar in his hand, the metal cool against his palm. Each round he loads is a promise, each target a piece of the war he's preparing for.

He fires, the suppressor muffling the shots to soft thumps, the recoil a steady pulse like his own heartbeat. The targets destroyed one-by-one, holes blooming in their centers, precise and lethal. Preach moves fast, his body a machine again, his mind locked on the rhythm of aim, fire, reload. He's trained for this, war, vengeance, survival, and the muscle memory is a comfort, a tether to the man he used to be, before Sarah, before the Slayers, before his world turned to ash.

The sky darkens, a lightning storm gathering in the distance, its flashes painting the horizon in jagged streaks of white. The air hums with electricity, the promise of rain heavy on the wind. Preach pauses, his breath steady, and checks his watch. The time glows in stark digits: 11:16. He stares at it, the numbers meaningless yet heavy, like a familiar secret code.

"Trouble's here," he whispers, his voice swallowed by the wind, as he loads another magazine. His hands are steady, his heart set on the fight he knows is coming. The storm rumbles closer, its thunder a drumbeat to match the one in his chest, and Preach fires again, the targets dying like soldiers in a war that's already begun.

9 - NOMAD

Killerton Parish hums with the restless pulse of the coast, its air thick with the briny tang of saltwater and the faint, sour decay of marshland reeds. The town sprawls along the shoreline, a patchwork of weathered clapboard houses and sun-bleached shops, their signs hawking fried shrimp, seashell necklaces, and faded postcards. Seagulls perch on cracked wooden railings along the boardwalk, their cries sharp against the constant crash of waves, a rhythm that feels like a warning, like the town itself is holding its breath. Dusk settles over the beach, painting the sky in bruised purples and oranges, as Preach drives a rented car with tinted windows through the narrow streets. The car's dark paint blends into the lengthening shadows, unremarkable, invisible, just the way he likes it. His eyes, hidden behind sunglasses, track the road ahead, locking onto a house tucked behind a low dune, its windows glowing with dim yellow light, curtains drawn tight like a secret.

Preach pulls into the lot of a seaside motel, a low-slung building with peeling white paint and a sign that buzzes faintly, its letters half-lit. He requests a corner room on the south side, second floor. His voice low, polite but firm, offering the clerk a folded $50 bill to avoid questions. The room is sparse: a single bed with a sagging mattress, a chipped wooden desk, and windows that rattle in the sea breeze, letting in the scent of salt and something wilder, older. It's 750 yards to Kane's house, close enough to strike, far enough to vanish. Preach sets up his gear with the precision of a soldier: a pair of binoculars on the desk, a notebook already thick with scribbled observations, and a map of Killerton Parish spread out like a battlefield, red ink circling Kane's haunts, his house, the bar he frequents, the pier where he meets his crew. For days, Preach watches, perched at the window, his body still as stone, his mind sharp as a blade. Kane moves like clockwork, leaving at dawn, returning near ten, his leather vest a constant, the "SLAYERS" patch bold against the black, a beacon of everything Preach has come to destroy. Case and Chase, the twins, are never far, their identical faces set in hard lines, their motorcycle parked in Kane's driveway like sentinels standing watch.

"You're a creature of habit, Kane," Preach mutters, his pen scratching against the notebook, marking the time Kane rolls in each night, always with a six-pack or a bottle of whiskey. The twins trailing in just before midnight. "Makes this too damn easy."

By day, Preach blends into Killerton Parish, a shadow in a faded ball cap and sunglasses, sipping coffee at a diner called Salty's, where the air smells of grease and burnt toast. Locals chatter over chipped mugs, their voices a low hum of fishing hauls, incoming storms, and the Slayers' latest trouble. "Heard they're stirring up shit again," a waitress named Margie says to a trucker, her voice hushed, her eyes darting to the door as she wipes the counter with a rag. "Kane's got them running something big. Drugs, probably. Always is."

Preach keeps his head down, stirring his coffee, the spoon clinking softly against the white mug. "What kind of trouble?" he asks, his tone light, like he's just another tourist passing through, curious but harmless.

Margie shrugs, her movements quick, nervous, like she's said too much already. "Drugs, fights, women, you name it. They're always into something. Stay clear of them, honey, unless you want trouble." She moves off to refill another customer's cup, her sneakers squeaking on the linoleum.

Preach nods, filing the information away, his mind running through the plans, traps, escape routes, contingencies, each one a thread in the web he's weaving. The Slayers are a cancer, and Kane is the heart of it. Preach knows what he has to do, has known it since the day Kane took Sarah, broke her, left her hollowed out and lost to the drugs he peddled. The memory burns, a coal in his chest, fueling every thought.

At night, he recons, his training guiding his steps through the shadows, his boots silent on the sandy paths that wind through Killerton Parish. The marsh nearby catches his eye, a secluded pocket of land surrounded by tall reeds and shallow, brackish water, a sandbar jutting out like a hidden stage. The ground is soft, treacherous, the kind of place where a man could disappear without a trace. He spends an hour sketching its layout in his notebook, noting the narrow trails, the shifting mud, the places where the reeds grow thick enough to hide a body. It's perfect, a natural choke point, a trap waiting to be sprung.

"You thinking of fishing out there?" a local asks, an older man with a sunburned face, spotting Preach near the marsh, his sketchbook in hand, his pencil moving quickly.

Preach flashes an easy smile, disarming, the kind that puts people at ease. "Just scoping out the scenery. Nice spot for some clamming, maybe."

The man grunts, unconvinced but uninterested, his eyes squinting against the sun. "It's dangerous out there, real soft. Watch your step, fella." He wanders off, his flip-flops slapping against the sand, leaving Preach alone with his plans.

On the third night, at 11:16 p.m., Preach makes his move. The sky is heavy with clouds, the air electric with the threat of a storm, distant thunder rumbling like a warning drum. He slips through the dunes to Kane's house, his silhouette a ghost against the night. The backdoor is unlocked, a careless mistake, and Preach eases it open, stepping into the kitchen. The TV blares from the living room, a late-night show, canned laughter echoing through the small house. Kane sits in an armchair, a beer in his hand, his back to the door, oblivious, the TV's glow casting jagged shadows across his face, his leather vest slung over the couch beside him.

Preach steps forward, silent on the worn carpet, his heart steady despite the adrenaline clawing through his veins. "You shouldn't have come between us, Kane," he says, his voice low, deliberate, like a blade wrapped in velvet.

Kane spins his head around, his eyes widening, the beer bottle slipping from his hand and hitting the floor, foam hissing across the carpet. "Preach? How the fuck did you get in here without me knowing?"

Preach's lips curl into a cold smile. "Because you've got the survival instincts of a breadcrumb, and now your ass is toast."

Kane lunges, his fist swinging, a wild haymaker aimed at Preach's jaw. But Preach is faster, his training kicking in, his body moving like a machine impervious to pain. He sidesteps, grabbing Kane's arm and twisting, forcing him back into the chair with a grunt. The room erupts into chaos, a brutal dance of fists and fury. Kane is strong, his punches heavy, his breath hot with rage as he lands a blow to Preach's arm, the impact jarring but not enough to slow him.

"You think you can just walk in here?" Kane growls, his voice thick, his fist swinging again, catching Preach's ribs with a dull thud.

Preach absorbs the hit, his eyes burning, his own fists answering with precision. He drives a punch into Kane's gut, doubling him over, then grabs his arm, twisting it behind his back. "You took her from me," Preach says, his voice shaking with rage, the words raw, torn from somewhere deep. "Got her hooked, broke her, broke us!"

Kane's face is red, his voice hoarse as he struggles against Preach's grip. "She wanted it, Preach! She came to me, begging for a hit, for a good time. You left her, man. You did this!"

The words cut, sharp as a knife, but Preach's hands find Kane's neck, his grip fierce, unyielding. "You don't get to blame me," he says, his voice a low snarl, and with a sharp twist, a sickening snap, it's over. Kane slumps in the chair, his eyes staring blankly at the ceiling, wide and unseeing, his body still, the TV's laughter a mocking echo in the quiet house. Preach stands, his chest heaving, his hands trembling with the weight of what he's done. He grabs Kane's Slayers vest from the couch, a trophy, a piece of his vengeance. He looks at his watch, and slips out the backdoor, leaving the TV blaring, its noise a hollow cover for the silence of death.

As he crosses the yard, a voice cuts through the night, sharp and urgent. "Kane? Yo, boss, you in there?" It's Chase, calling from the front door, his boots heavy on the porch. Preach freezes in the shadows, his heart pounding, the vest clutched tight in his hand. Chase steps inside, his silhouette framed by the doorway, and then a yell tears through the night, raw with shock. "Kane! Oh, God, no!"

Chase's voice breaks as he finds the body, his footsteps heavy as he rushes to the chair, to Kane's lifeless form, his neck twisted at an unnatural angle.

Preach moves quickly, disappearing into the dunes, the sand swallowing his steps, the vest a heavy weight in his hands. He's back in his motel room before the first sirens wail in the distance, the ocean's restless rhythm a counterpoint to his racing pulse. He makes it a point to go to the front desk, and ask the clerk for towels. It's a rock solid alibi.

The next morning, Preach is at his window, sipping coffee from a styrofoam cup, the ocean stretching out below, its waves relentless against the shore. The twins are driving around asking the locals if they've seen any strangers in the area matching Preach's description. Margie from the diner points them towards the motel.

The twins' pickup roars into the motel lot, kicking up gravel. Case behind the wheel, his face twisted with rage as he scans the building. "I guarantee you it was that motherfucker Preach who killed Kane," Case says, his voice carrying through the open window, sharp with conviction, his hands gripping the steering wheel like he's choking it.

Chase, in the passenger seat, nods, his jaw tight, his eyes burning with the same fire. "We'll get him, Case. He's a dead man walking."

They circle the lot, their horn blaring, a sharp, deliberate sound meant to draw attention. Preach saw them coming a mile away, his instincts honed, his plan already shifting to account for their rage. He steps to the window, sliding the curtain aside for a clear view. The twins spot him, their eyes locking onto his, and both raise their middle fingers, a silent promise of retribution. Preach nods, a small, deliberate gesture, his face unreadable as they peel out, the truck's engine roaring like a challenge.

He turns back to the room, his gaze drifting to the ocean, its surface churned by the wind, whitecaps breaking against the shore. A large man walks the boardwalk below, his frame broad, his stride purposeful, his presence like a storm cloud moving across the horizon. Their eyes meet briefly, a fleeting moment that feels like a warning, like the air before a lightning strike. Preach doesn't know him, but something about the man's gaze feels familiar, like a memory he can't place, a shadow from another time. He files it away, another piece of the puzzle, another threat to consider.

Later, Preach leaves the motel, his steps sinking into the cool sand as he walks along the beach, the wind tugging at his jacket. He finds the secluded marsh again, its sandbar a hidden pocket surrounded by reeds and shallow water, the ground soft and treacherous underfoot. "Perfect," he whispers, his mind already mapping out traps, tripwires in the reeds, choke points on the narrow trails, places where the mud could slow a pursuer. He's alone in this war against the Slayers, a one-man army fueled by rage and loss, but he's ready. His training is a shield, his vengeance a blade, and Killerton Parish, with its restless waves and hidden marshes, is the battlefield where he'll make his stand.

10 - REMORSE

Preach is heading downstairs to checkout. The clerk at the Killerton Parish hotel barely lifts her eyes from the glossy pages of her magazine as he slides the key across the counter. Her fingers, tipped with chipped red polish, snatch it up without a word, her attention fixed on a headline about celebrity breakups. Preach adjusts the duffel bag slung over his shoulder, the weight of it grounding him as he steps out into the humid morning air. The parking lot shimmers under the August sun, heat rising in waves from the asphalt, and he squints against the glare. He gets into the rental car, and heads back home. The road to Ironholler stretches ahead, a ribbon of black cutting through fields of swaying grass and dense pine forests, the horizon blurring into a haze of green and gold. He frequently checks his rearview mirror to make sure he's not followed by anyone. His mind lingers on the events in Killerton Parish. His business there is far from over. The Slayers burn in his thoughts, remnants of a fight he didn't start but can't walk away from.

Ironholler greets him with its familiar quiet, the kind of stillness that feels like it's holding its breath. Main Street is a sleepy stretch of mom-and-pop shops, their faded signs creaking in the breeze. He's passing the old hardware store when he sees him, the large man from Killerton Parish, his broad frame unmistakable even among the cluster of pedestrians at the crosswalk. The man moves with a deliberate ease, his dark coat brushing the backs of his knees. Their eyes lock, a fleeting moment that feels like it stretches into eternity, a silent conversation heavy with unspoken questions. Preach's grip tightens on the steering wheel, a chill crawling up his spine despite the warm day. The man's gaze is unyielding, not hostile but piercing, like he sees straight through to the scars Preach carries inside. The light turns green, Preach drives on leaving the moment behind, but not the weight of it.

"Who is that guy?" he mutters to himself, the words lost in the rush of air from the open car windows. "Seen him a couple places before. What's his deal?"

The question dogs him as he drives on. He's seen the man twice now, once at the motel in Killerton Parish, and now here, in Ironholler, blending into the crowd yet standing apart. There's something about him, something Preach can't place, like a shadow that moves just out of sight.

In Killerton Parish, the twins are plotting. Case and Chase huddle in the dim light of their garage, the air thick with the smell of oil and stale cigarettes. Their voices are low, urgent, their grief for Kane a raw wound that festers with every word. "Preach took him from us," Case says, his voice a growl, his knuckles white around a wrench. "He's gonna pay. Blood for blood."

Chase nods, his eyes burning with the same fire, his fingers tracing the outline of an automatic rifle on the workbench. "We hit him wherever we see him first. End this quick."

Case slams the wrench down, the clang echoing through the garage. "No mistakes, Chase. We do this for Kane."

Oblivious to the twins' plans, Preach rides back into Killerton Parish the next day, the Ace of Spades humming beneath him as he pulls into the gravel lot of the Burger Joint on the edge of town. The sign spelling out "EAT" in a flickering glow. He parks the bike, the engine ticking as it cools, and steps inside, the bell above the door jingling. The place is alive with the chatter of families, kids laughing over milkshakes, the jukebox crooning an old country tune. The smell of fries and sizzling bacon wraps around him, familiar and comforting, a brief respite from the war that's consumed him. He slides onto a stool at the counter, nodding to the waitress, a woman with tired eyes and a quick smile.

"Hey darling, what can I get you?" as she takes out her scratch pad.

"Let me get a burger, medium, extra pickles," he says, his voice rough from the road. "And a sweet tea."

She winks, tucking a strand of graying hair behind her ear. "You got it hon, coming right up."

He leans back, his eyes drifting to the window, his mind on something else. The Slayers picked this fight, but he's the one finishing it. His fingers tap the counter, then the world erupts.

Gunfire rips through the windows, glass shattering in a cascade of shards that glint in the sunlight. Screams pierce the air, the jukebox cutting off mid-verse, music replaced by chaos. Preach dives, instinct taking over, his body hitting the floor as he grabs a little boy from a nearby booth, pulling him to safety behind a table. The boy's eyes are wide, his breath coming in panicked gasps, his small hands clutching Preach's jacket. "Stay down!" Preach says, his voice calm despite the pounding in his chest, his arms wrapping around the boy like a shield. "It's okay, kid. I got you."

The boy whimpers, his face buried in Preach's chest. "I want my mom," he says, his voice trembling.

"She's right over there, see?" Preach nods toward a woman crouched behind another table, her eyes locked on her son, her hands pressed to her mouth. "She's safe. You're safe. Just sit tight."

The clock on the wall reads 11:16, and Preach's heart skips, that number a curse that's haunted him forever. He peers over the table, his eyes scanning the chaos outside. The twins' pickup truck roars in the lot, Chase in the bed, his automatic rifle spitting fire, the muzzle flashes bright against the daylight. Case is behind the wheel, his face a mask of rage, his hands steady as they haul ass in the truck.

"Who the hell was that?" a man yells from behind a booth, his voice shaking as he clutches his wife's hand.

Preach doesn't answer, his focus on the scene outside. Then he sees him again, that large man, the Nomad, moving like a flash, grabbing the Ace of Spades from the lot and tearing after the truck. The bike's engine screams, a feral sound that cuts through the gunfire. A bullet grazes the gas tank, but the Nomad doesn't falter, his body low over the handlebars, his eyes locked on the truck. In a single fluid motion, he pulls a large knife from under the back of his coat, and throws it. The blade catches the sunlight as it spins through the air and buries itself in Chase's chest. Chase's body jerks, he drops the rifle and he falls off the back of the truck, slamming onto the pavement as Case speeds away, his shout of fury audible even over the engine's roar.

The Nomad stops the bike beside Chase's body. He retrieves his knife with a quick tug, and vanishes into the wind, his coat billowing as he slips away. Preach runs outside, the boy now clinging to his mother, her sobs of relief echoing in his ears. An idling car sits in the lot, its owner screaming from the sidewalk. Preach doesn't hesitate, sliding into the driver's seat and peeling out, the tires screeching as he follows the trail of the Ace of Spades.

About half a mile away, he finds it parked on the side of the road with the engine still running. The air heavy with the scent of exhaust and blood, and no other cars in sight. Chase lies dead, his eyes staring blankly at the sky, his vest stained red with his own blood. Preach kneels beside him, his breath heavy, and slides the leather vest off Chase's body. It's heavier than he expected, the weight of it more than just leather and thread. Another trophy, another marker in this endless war. He tucks it into his saddlebag, his eyes scanning the empty road. The Nomad is gone, like he was never there. Preach takes off on the Ace of Spades.

That night, under a moonless sky, Preach moves through the shadows toward the Slayers' clubhouse in Ironholler. The air is thick with the scent of gasoline, the clubhouse a squat building, its windows glowing faintly. He drops Kane and Chase's vests in the dirt, a sign of total disrespect, and douses them with lighter fluid. He takes a silver lighter from his pocket, and flips it across his thigh. He lights the vests on fire, flames leap up casting dancing shadows on the clubhouse walls. The fire crackles, a hungry sound that fills the silence, and Preach steps back into the shadows, his heart pounding, his hands steady.

The door bursts open, and the remaining eight Slayers spill out, their voices a symphony of rage and fear, their guns drawn as they scan the darkness. "Who the fuck did this?" one shouts, a wiry man with a shaved head, his pistol shaking in his hand.

"You bastard!" another yells, his voice cracking, his shotgun sweeping the shadows.

Preach revs the Ace of Spades, the engine's roar a challenge that cuts through their shouts. He tears off into the night, the bike's tire squealing away. The Slayers give chase, as Preach purposely leads them into Killerton Parish. Preach makes it back to the old hotel parking lot. He parks the bike, making sure the Slayers see him. He runs into the marsh. The ground turns soft beneath his feet, the air heavy with the scent of salt and decay, the reeds whispering in the breeze. He's prepared for this, every trap set with precision, tripwires hidden in the mud, explosives buried beneath the sandbar, each one a silent promise of retribution.

The Slayers chase him like rabid wolves, and one-by-one, they fall. A tripwire snaps, and an explosion tears through the night, a man's scream cut short as the blast consumes him. Another steps on a pressure plate, and a hidden blade swings from the reeds, silencing him before he can cry out. The marsh swallows their screams, the darkness hiding their bodies, until only Case remains, his eyes wild, his knife beaming in the moonlight as he faces Preach on the sandbar.

"You killed my twin brother, a part of me!" Case snarls, circling Preach, his knife glinting with every step, his voice thick with grief and rage. "You killed Kane. You're a dead man."

Preach is firm, his stance steady, his eyes cold. "You brought this on yourself, Case," he says, his voice low, unyielding. "You all did. You think I wanted this? You think I needed any of this?"

Case lunges, his knife slicing through the air, narrowly missing Preach's arm. Preach doesn't flinch, he's a well trained machine. They clash, a brutal dance of fists and steel, the sand shifting beneath their boots, the air heavy with the scent of blood and salt. Case is fast, his grief fueling him, but Preach is relentless, his movements precise, lethal. He steps back, draws a pistol, and fires a single shot. Case clutches his throat with both hands, blood seeping through his fingers. His eyes widen, a gasp escaping his lips as he falls, his dead body crumpling in the water. The moonlight sparkling as his body drifts away into the dark ocean.

Suddenly, the Nomad steps from the shadows, his presence calm, almost otherworldly. "Any remorse for what you've done?" he asks, his voice low, resonant, like a prayer carried on the wind.

Preach collapses to his knees, the weight of it all crashing over him like a wave. Tears stream down his face, hot and unrelenting, his hands shaking as he clutches the pistol. "God, forgive me," he sobs, his voice raw, breaking. "I didn't want this. I just wanted her back, wanted my life back. Please, forgive me, Lord!"

The Nomad stands beside him, his hand resting on Preach's shoulder, firm and steady, a lifeline in the dark. "You are forgiven," he says, the words simple but heavy, settling deep in Preach's soul, a balm to the wounds he's carried for too long. Preach's sobs quiet, the marsh silent around them as the Nomad's hand lingers, a silent vow that he's not alone.

11 - DAYSTAR

The marsh stretches wide and wild around Preach, it's expanse a living, breathing thing, pulsing with the hum of unseen creatures and the rustle of reeds swaying in the dawn's gentle breeze. The air carries the sharp tang of salt and decay, a scent that clings to his skin, heavy and unyielding. In his hand, the gun barrel is still warm, a silent testament to the violence that has shadowed his life, its weight grounding him to this moment on the sandbar. Above, the sky burns with the first light of morning, pale pinks and golds bleeding into the blue horizon, a canvas of fleeting beauty that feels almost cruel in its indifference to the blood on his hands.

Beside him stands the Nomad, his silhouette sharp against the vibrant sky, his long dark coat flapping lightly in the wind like the wings of some ancient bird. His face is weathered, etched with lines that speak of stories untold, but his eyes hold a quiet strength, a kindness that feels both ancient and immediate, as if he's seen the world's beginning and its end and chosen to linger here, in this moment, for Preach. The Nomad's boots sink slightly into the damp sand, his presence as solid as the earth itself, and when he speaks, his voice is a low rumble, deliberate, like stones settling into a riverbed.

"That time you keep seeing, Napoleon. 11:16. It's not a curse, not some ghost haunting your days," the Nomad says, his gaze fixed on Preach, unyielding but not unkind. "It's a reminder. Psalm 91:11. 'For he shall order his angels to guard you wherever you go.' I've been with you since you took your first breath, dispatched by your father. You think all those near misses in your life were luck? That car when you were eight, riding your bike down the street, swerving just before it would've hit you? The fall from that elm tree, not a single bone broken? The house fire that killed both your parents, but you and Keisha were unharmed, right? I was there, protecting you."

Preach's breath catches in his throat, sharp and jagged, like he's swallowed glass. His eyes, red-rimmed and stinging with unshed tears, lock onto the Nomad's face, searching for some crack in the truth, some hint of deception. But there's none, only that steady gaze, those flecks of gold in the Nomad's irises catching the dawn's light. "You?" Preach's voice is a whisper, barely audible over the rustle of the reeds, trembling with disbelief and something deeper, something like awe. "All this time?"

The Nomad nods, his expression unchanging, as if he's confirming the rising of the sun. "Every moment you saw 11:16, I was there shielding you, keeping you safe. You remember that day in the desert, when the insurgents had you pinned down, bullets kicking up sand all around you? The raggedy helicopter that distracted them, drawing their fire? Who do you think started the engine?"

Preach shakes his head, his mind a storm of memories, each one flashing like lightning across a dark sky. He's eight again, pedaling down a cracked asphalt street, the screech of tires and the blur of a car's bumper missing him by inches. He's ten, tumbling from the highest branch of the old elm tree in his backyard, landing hard but whole, his heart pounding as Keisha's screams echoed from the porch. He's thirteen, coughing through smoke as flames devoured the house, Keisha's hand in his, both of them stumbling out into the night while their parents' screams faded into silence. Then the war, the endless firefights, bullets whining past his head, the numbers 11:16 glaring at him from a shattered watch on a dead man's wrist, from a gas pump, from license plates. Always that number, a shadow he thought was an omen.

"I thought…" His voice cracks, and he swallows hard, trying to steady it, his throat raw as if he's been screaming. "I thought it was just chance. Or God."

"It was both," the Nomad says, his tone softening, a warmth threading through his words like sunlight through a cracked window. "God works through us, Napoleon. Through me. Through you. You've carried a heavy burden, but you've never been alone."

Preach's hands tremble, the pistol slipping from his grip to rest in the water, its metal dull in the morning light. The weight of it pulls at him, a reminder of the lives he's taken, their faces flashing in his mind: Kane, his eyes wide with betrayal as life left his body; the rest of the Slayers, all dead. So many others, their images a litany of guilt that haunts his dreams. His voice breaks as he speaks, raw and ragged. "I've killed, so many. Kane, all the rest… I can still see their faces, every one of them. How can I be forgiven for that? How can I stand before God with all this blood on my hands?"

The Nomad kneels, his coat pooling around him like spilled ink, his eyes level with Preach's, close enough that Preach can see the quiet certainty in them, a depth that feels like it could swallow the world. "You fought for what you believed was right," the Nomad says, his voice steady but laced with compassion, like a father speaking to a wounded son. "You carried the weight of those choices, and you've seen the cost. You've asked for forgiveness, Napoleon, and it was granted. But now you stand at a crossroads. Will you serve him?"

Tears spill down Preach's cheeks, hot and unchecked, carving tracks through the grime and salt on his face. His chest heaves, each breath a struggle, as if his heart is fighting to break free from the cage of his ribs. He thinks of the marsh, this wild, untamed place that feels like a mirror to his soul, and the sky above, vast and unjudging. "I'm done with the killing," he says, his voice raw but resolute, a vow carved into the air between them. "I swear it, I'll serve Him. I'll make it right, whatever it takes. I promise. I'll bury the old me, because I know if he gets out, hell is coming with him. I can only do this if God changes my heart."

The Nomad's expression softens, the lines around his eyes crinkling, and he reaches into the pocket of his coat. He pulls out a playing card, its edges crisp and unblemished, the green pattern of suits on the back, and on the front, the Ace of Spades unmistakable in the dawn's light. He presses it into Preach's hand, his fingers warm and steady against Preach's trembling ones. "Kept this safe for you," the Nomad says, his voice low, almost tender.

Preach stares at the card, his fingers tracing its edges, the familiar weight of it pulling him back to a different time. He's in the desert again, the air thick with dust and heat, his platoon gathered around him. This exact card, the Ace of Spades, was in his pocket during the battle where they'd all made it home, unscathed, against impossible odds, a talisman of survival. "I thought I lost this, how did you…?" he starts, his voice faltering, the question hanging unfinished in the air.

"The burden is not yours, never was." the Nomad says, his voice resonant, like a bell tolling in the distance. "This card, it's a piece of who you were. A reminder of the men you fought for, all came home alive because of you, your faith. You have a new path now, Napoleon. A better one."

Preach nods, his tears falling onto the sand, soaking into the earth like an offering. "I will," he says, his voice steadier now, a vow not just to the Nomad but to himself, to the God he's spent years running from. "I choose it."

The Nomad smiles, a rare, fleeting thing, like sunlight breaking through a storm cloud. "Then you're already on that path."

Preach wipes his face and asks the Nomad, "Do you have a name?"

"Damon." the Nomad says in a comforting tone. "It's Damon Legna." He then points to the blue sky above. "Look up, Napoleon."

Preach raises his eyes, and in that instant, the Nomad is gone, vanished as if he'd never been there at all. The marsh is silent, the reeds still, the air heavy with the absence of his presence. Above, a shooting star streaks across the sky, a rare Daystar, its light piercing with brilliance that feels like a promise. Preach's breath catches, his heart swelling with a clarity he's never known, a sense of purpose settling into his bones like a fire kindled in the dark.

He stands, the sandbar shifting beneath his boots, the Ace of Spades card clutched tightly in his hand. The bodies that littered the sandbar moments ago, are gone, washed away into the sea as if they were never there, as if the marsh itself has swallowed his sins. The air hums with the drone of insects, the distant cry of a gull cutting through the stillness. Preach whispers a prayer, his voice low but steady, the words carrying a weight he's only beginning to understand. "Lord, guide me," he says, his eyes fixed on the fading trail of the Daystar. "Show me the way."

The dawn breaks fully over the horizon, painting the sky in hues of gold and crimson, and Preach feels something shift inside him, a lightness, childlike hope he thought he'd lost forever. The card in his hand is a tether to his past, but also a bridge to what comes next. He tucks it into his pocket, the motion deliberate, and turns away from the sandbar. The marsh stretches out before him, alive and untamed, a new beginning waiting to be claimed.

His boots crunch against the sand as he makes his way back to the parking lot, where his motorcycle waits, its chrome sparkling in the risen sun. He swings a leg over, the leather seat creaking under his weight, and fires up the engine. The rumble vibrates through him, a familiar pulse that feels like an extension of his heartbeat. The road ahead stretches toward home, toward a life he's only beginning to imagine. He glances at the sky one last time, the Daystar's trail now faded, but its promise lingers in his mind. With a twist of the throttle, he pulls onto the road, Killerton Parish falling away behind him, his journey back to Ironholler a different one, shaped by the weight of a vow and the lightness of grace.

12 - NEW BEGINNINGS

Years later, the sanctuary of New Beginnings Church in Ironholler hums with life, the air thick with the scent of polished wood and the faint sweetness of hymnals stacked neatly in the pews. Sunlight streams through the stained-glass windows, casting shards of red, blue, and gold across the congregation, their faces upturned, voices weaving through the final notes of "Amazing Grace." The wooden rafters above seem to hold the song, letting it linger like a prayer. Preach stands behind the pulpit, his pastor's robe a stark contrast to the fatigues of his past, its black fabric simple yet heavy with purpose. His hands, once calloused from gripping a rifle, now rest gently on the worn edges of his Bible, its pages marked with years of study and reflection. He surveys the room, eyes warm, crinkling at the corners as he smiles at the faces before him, young and old, each carrying their own burdens, their own hopes.

"Brothers and sisters," Preach begins, his voice steady, resonant, filling the sanctuary without effort, "today we gather not just to worship, but to welcome new souls into God's family. Let's head outside, where the River Jordan's waters are waiting."

The congregation rises, a rustle of movement, their footsteps soft on the hardwood floor as they spill into the churchyard. Behind the church, under the shade of a sprawling oak, two metal beer tubs bask in the sunlight, filled with water that ripples gently in the breeze. They're unconventional, sure, but Preach likes them that way, a nod to Ironholler's rough edges, a reminder that salvation doesn't need polish to be real. A young woman named Lila steps forward, her sundress clinging to her thin frame, her eyes bright with tears she doesn't try to hide. She's barely twenty, her life a tangle of mistakes she's ready to leave behind. Preach kneels next to the tub, the water warm against his arms, and extends a hand to her.

"You ready, Lila?" he asks, his voice soft, steady, like a father speaking to a child.

She nods, her lips trembling, her hands twisting together. "I'm scared, Pastor. What if... what if I'm not good enough?"

Preach's smile is gentle, his eyes holding hers, unwavering. "Ain't none of us good enough, sister. That's why it's called grace. God don't ask for perfect, just willing. Are you willing?"

Her breath catches, and she nods again, stronger this time. "Yes. I'm willing."

He guides her into the water, his hands steady on her shoulders. "Then let's do this." He speaks the words of baptism, his voice carrying over the murmur of the crowd, their faces a blur of anticipation and joy. "In the name of the Father, the Son, and the Holy Spirit..." He lowers her gently, the water closing over her, and when she rises, gasping, her face is alight, her smile radiant, her wet hair clinging to her cheeks.

"Welcome to the family," Preach says, his hands still on her shoulders, grounding her in the moment. "You're home now."

Lila's voice trembles, but there's strength in it, a spark that wasn't there before. "Thank you, Pastor. I never thought I'd find this. Never thought I could."

He chuckles, the sound warm, easing the weight of the moment. "God finds us all, sister. You just gotta listen when He calls."

The crowd erupts in cheers, clapping and hollering, some wiping tears of their own. Preach helps Lila out of the tub, handing her a towel as another member steps forward, ready for their turn. The baptisms continue, each one a story unfolding, each soul a step closer to redemption. The churchyard buzzes with energy, children darting through the grass, their laughter mingling with the sizzle of ribs on the grill nearby. The air carries the tang of barbecue sauce, the sweetness of cornbread, and the faint smokiness of charcoal, blending into a scent that feels like home.

As the baptisms wind down, Preach steps away from the tubs, wiping his hands on a rag, his robe damp at the hem. The first Sunday of the month means more than baptisms; it's the day of the BBQ Motorcycle Mission Ride, a tradition he started years ago, when he realized the open road could carry faith as easily as it once carried his anger. He heads toward the lot where the bikes are parked, their chrome catching the sun, a row of gleaming machines that roar with purpose. The Ace of Spades, his trusty steed sits at the front, its polished shine, the Ace of Spades playing card painted on the tank with that blemish, a symbol of the man he used to be, and the man he's become.

"Pastor!" a voice calls, rough and familiar. Dolo, a burly biker with a graying beard and a leather vest patched with years of rides, strides over, a grin splitting his face. "You leading us to salvation or just to the best ribs in Ironholler?"

Preach laughs, the sound deep and warm, filling the air as he adjusts his helmet. "Both, Dolo. Man can't live by bread alone."

Dolo claps him on the shoulder, his eyes twinkling with mischief. "Long as you don't make me sing no hymns out there. My pipes are better suited for cussing than choruses."

"Deal," Preach says, swinging a leg over his bike. "But I'm holding you to a prayer at the pit stop."

Dolo groans, but it's playful, his grin never fading. "You're a hard man, Pastor. Hard man."

The other bikers gather, a mix of grizzled veterans and younger riders, some with vests a patchwork of club insignias and Bible verses stitched in white thread. They're a rough crowd, some still carrying the scars of their old lives, but they're here, drawn by Preach's message, by the promise of something bigger than themselves. He revs the Ace of Spades, the engine's rumble a call to action, and the others follow suit, the sound a symphony of power that shakes the ground.

"Ride with purpose!" Preach shouts over the noise, his voice carrying a fire that feels like it comes from somewhere deeper than his chest. "We ain't just ridin' for us, we're ridin' for Him! Luke 14:23 says

Go out to the Highways and Country roads. That's where we are headed, Saints."

The bikes roll out, kicking up gravel, the line stretching down the road like a ribbon of faith. They wind through the hills surrounding Ironholler, the asphalt flanked by fields of wildflowers, their colors a blur of yellow and purple, and stands of pine, their scent sharp and clean in the air. Preach leads, the wind whipping at his face, carrying away the shadows of his past. He feels alive out here, the road a path to something greater, each mile a prayer, each turn a chance to leave the old Preach behind.

They stop at a clearing overlooking the valley, the bikes idling as the riders dismount, stretching their legs, sharing stories over bottles of water and the occasional root beer. Preach leans against the Ace of Spades, listening as a young man named Caleb approaches, his boots crunching on the dirt. Caleb's barely out of his teens, his eyes clear now, his hands steady, a far cry from the shaking wreck he was when Preach first met him, strung out and running with the wrong crowd.

"Pastor," Caleb says, his voice low, almost shy, "can I talk to you a sec?"

"Always," Preach says, gesturing to a nearby rock where they can sit. The valley stretches out below them, green and gold in the afternoon light, the distant hum of the other riders' voices a soft backdrop. "What's on your mind?"

Caleb scuffs his boot in the dirt, his hands shoved in his pockets. "I just... I wanted to say thanks. For everything. I was lost, you know? Running with those dealers, heading nowhere fast. Everyone told me I'd end up dead, or in jail. Then you found me, showed me the way."

Preach shakes his head, his expression soft but firm. "Wasn't me, brother. That was God. I'm just the messenger, pointing you to the door. You're the one who walked through it."

Caleb's eyes glisten, but he blinks it away, nodding. "Still. You didn't give up on me. Not a lot of people would've bothered."

Preach pats a hand on Caleb's shoulder, his grip steady, reassuring. "That's what this is all about, Caleb. Not giving up on each other. You're family now. We got your back."

They sit in silence for a moment, the wind carrying the scent of pine and earth, the valley below a reminder of how far they've all come. Preach thinks of Sarah then, the ache in his chest a quiet companion he's learned to live with. She's still at the rehab facility, her recovery from the brain damage slow but steady, a fact he clings to in his prayers. He wonders if she's found peace, if she ever thinks of him, of the life they might've built together. Late at night, when the church is quiet and the stars burn bright over Ironholler, he prays for her, asking God to heal what he couldn't, to guide her to a place of light.

The ride back to the church is slower, the sun dipping low, painting the sky in hues of orange and pink. At the barbecue, the churchyard is alive again, tables laden with platters of ribs, coleslaw, and cornbread, the air thick with laughter and the clink of mason jars. Preach mingles, shaking hands, listening to stories of redemption, his presence a quiet anchor in the crowd. He's different now, the wrath and vengeance of his past buried deep, replaced by a purpose that burns brighter than any anger ever could.

"Hi Pastor." a voice calls, pulling him from his thoughts. It's an older woman named Ruth, her hair streaked with gray, her hands clutching a Bible, its cover worn, the edges frayed. She approaches slowly, her steps hesitant, her eyes downcast.

"Hello," Preach says, guiding her to a picnic bench under the oak, the chatter of the crowd fading to a soft hum around them. The smell of barbecue drifts on the breeze, mingling with the scent of grass and wildflowers. "What's on your mind, Ruth?"

She sits, her fingers tracing the Bible's cover, her voice barely above a whisper. "I did things I'm not proud of, Pastor. Things I can't take back. Things that... they haunt me, you know? Keep me up at night. Can God really forgive me for that?"

Preach leans forward, his elbows on his knees, his eyes meeting hers with a gentleness born of his own pain. "He forgave me, sister," he says, his words deliberate, weighted with truth. "And I've done worse than most. I was a soldier, Ruth. A killer. Carried that weight for years, thought it'd crush me. But God took it, made me a pastor instead. If He can do that for a man like me, He can forgive you. Just ask, and mean it."

Ruth's eyes fill with tears, her hands trembling as she clutches the Bible tighter. "I want to believe that," she whispers. "I want to so bad."

"Then let's pray," Preach says, his voice soft but sure. He takes her hand, bowing his head, their voices blending in a quiet prayer against the hum of the crowd. "Lord, you know Ruth's heart. You know her pain, her regrets. Show her your mercy, your love. Let her feel your forgiveness, and guide her to peace."

When they finish, Ruth's shoulders relax, her face softer, the weight she's carried seeming lighter, if only for a moment. "Thank you, Pastor," she says, her voice steadier now. "I think... I think I can try."

"That's all He asks," Preach says, smiling. "One step at a time."

The barbecue stretches into the evening, the sky darkening, the stars beginning to peek through. Preach moves through the crowd, his heart full, the shadows of his past finally at rest. The church grows, lives change, and he feels at peace, anchored in faith, the Ace of Spades parked under the oak a quiet reminder of the road he's traveled, and the man he's become. A flash of a star streaking across the sky, reminds him of something greater.

THE END
OF THE BEGINNING

Thank you for reading! If this book inspired or impacted you, please share it with others. For more books, quizzes, and information, or to show your support and explore exclusive apparel, visit our website.

www.DamonLegna.com

Epilogue

Preach sits on the porch of his Ironholler home, the Ace of Spades motorcycle parked in the driveway, its chrome catching the moonlight. The night is quiet, the stars bright above, a canvas of light that feels like a promise. He holds a Bible, its pages worn from years of reading, and opens it to Psalm 91:11 where the Ace of Spades playing card rests as a bookmark. The words etched into his soul. The clock inside chimes, a soft, familiar sound, and he glances at his watch: 11:16.

He smiles, unafraid, the number no longer a bad omen but a reminder, a sign of the angel who walked with him through fire and shadow. "Thank you," he whispers, his voice carrying into the night, a prayer of gratitude for the Nomad, for the forgiveness he's found, for the life he's built. Sarah is in rehab with a long recovery from brain damage caused by the drug overdose. Preach is hopeful, as he knows God has a plan for her.

The wind stirs, carrying the scent of pine and earth, and Preach leans back, his eyes on the stars. Somewhere, he knows, Damon Legna watches, and he feels a peace that settles deep, ready for whatever comes next, his heart steady, his soul at rest.